River of Milk 'n Honey

by William W. Thackeray

*Best regards,
William W.
Thackeray*

Wild Coyote Publications

First Edition edited by
Wild Coyote Publications, Box 985,
Chinook, MT 59523.
Copyright © 2004 by William W. Thackeray

Cover: Homestead School, near Havre.
From the Al Lucke Collection,
Montana Historical Society.

ISBN: 1-59152-015-0

This book may not be reproduced in whole or in part
by any means (with the exception of short quotes for the
purpose of review) without the permission of the publisher.

Produced by Farcountry Press,
P.O. Box 5630, Helena, MT 59602
www.farcountrypress.com
800-821-3874

Printed in Canada

*Dedicated to
Bonnie, Martha,
Linde, Stephanie
and Will
For their help!*

Chapter 1

MATRICULATION

"Goddammit," Buddy said, "The cards are for shit today."

He threw his cards in and stood up. He was wearing a large blue dress covered with pink roses. He had a pillow strapped around his waist under the dress so he would look like a fat old lady. A pair of old lady's lace-up shoes with large heels loaned to the school by my grandma caused him to move with comical awkwardness.

We were sitting around the overshoes box in the cloakroom of Burnham School, playing poker for matches at a penny a match. In the classroom we could hear the shrill voices of the girls and the teacher, Mrs. Swift, singing "Home on the Range." It was eighth grade graduation day.

"Sit down," I said. "It ain't the cards that are for shit. It's you. You're just afraid to bet, 'cuz you might loose a coupla matches."

"To hell with you," Buddy said. He walked to the front door of the school and threw it open. It was early May but a wisp of snow blew across the floor. A cold gust of wind blew under the old lady dresses we were wearing.

"For Christ sake," Ernie yelled. "Shut the goddam door. Were you born in a barn!" Ernie took the card game and everything else super seriously. "Gimme two cards," he scratched his cards on the slivery cover of the overshoes box and tossed two cards into the discard pile.

"He's got three of a kind and wants a pair of aces," I droned tossing him two cards from the top of the worn deck.

"He's got three one-eyes and wants two more." Buddy had closed the door and was looking over Ernie's shoulder.

"Shit, man, don't snoop in my hand," Ernie said. He turned his hand down and wouldn't look at his draw until Buddy had moved back to his place across the table from me.

"I suppose you're out," I said to Buddy.

"Hell, no, I'm not out. After I seen what Ernie had, I'm gonna stay 'til the last dog is dead." Buddy gathered up his hand from the discard pile and tossed four cards back into discard. "Gimme the goddam four aces you were too cheap to give Ernie."

"You're out," Ernie said with menace in his voice. "You can't throw yer cards away and then expect to draw to them."

"To hell with you," Buddy said. "What you mean is you can't draw cards until you've thrown your discard away. I threw my discard away, so gimme four cards."

I shrugged and dealt four cards onto the table.

Ernie put his hand over the four cards. "You threw yer hand away and, by God, that means you're out." He reared back from the table and stared across at Buddy. There was a long quiet moment.

"Jeez, you guys," Lyle said, "Let's finish this hand before we have to go back in." Lyle was the fourth player, sitting on the floor to my right. He was the oldest one of us and wore the same bib overalls and cheap plaid shirt he wore every day. In the comic graduation skit we were in, he was playing the old farmer in a household of three fat old ladies who sat around and complained and gossiped all day while he did the work. Mrs. Swift had him play the farmer because she knew she could never get him into another costume. Besides, the farmer only had three lines to memorize. Mrs. Swift was probably afraid Lyle would have trouble remembering even those.

"So how many cards do you need?" I asked him, trying to get past the challenge.

"Shit, he's too dumb to know how many cards he wants," Buddy said. Although he was speaking to Lyle, he didn't take his eyes off Ernie.

"Goddam you, Buddy, I told you to leave Lyle alone," Ernie said. "He can't help it he's not goin' to graduate." It was an open secret that Lyle was going to go through the graduation ceremony without really graduating. But this was the first time anybody had mentioned it in front of Lyle.

"He's dumb as a fuckin' post," Buddy said, with his eyes still fixed on Ernie.

I looked at Lyle. He was sitting with his head down and tears dripped onto his red plaid shirt.

"Je-ezus Christ," I said. "You mean bastards, lay off Lyle and play cards. Buddy, you threw your damn hand away, so Ernie's right. You're out and I shouldn't have given you any cards. Now, help Lyle with his goddam discard so we can finish this fuckin' hand."

"Christ, the squirt's gitting a real mouth on him," Buddy said. But he looked at Lyle's hand and tossed two cards into the discard pile.

"The dummy bets three matches," he added throwing three matches from Lyle's pile into the pot.

"Wait 'til I draw," I said. "I need three cards, but I'll match you with three big ones." I tossed three matches from my pile into the pot.

"Are you with us, Ernie," I asked. He was still staring at Buddy. "Christ," I said, "let's just finish this hand and graduate."

Ernie looked at his hand again and tossed three matches into the pot. "So the big shot is joining the army, so he thinks he can kick everybody's ass before he goes. So whatcha' gonna do, hero, dig fuckin' foxholes and fill 'em up for the next four years." Now he was ignoring Buddy while he talked about him.

"Nah, I'm gonna be in army school in Hawaii while you poor bastards freeze your asses off here in Montana," Buddy responded cheerfully. I was glad his tone suggested the fight was over.

"So what's everybody got for cards?" I threw my hand face up on the table. I had a pair of sixes and not much else.

"I gotcha with two queens," Ernie said, reaching for the pot.

"Hold it, you smart-assed old ladies. Our dumb friend here has three fours. I believe that cleans you out," Buddy said. "Grab your pot, Farmer Brown," he told Lyle. Farmer Brown was the character Lyle was playing in the graduation skit. "And you better remember your goddam lines today, so the parents can celebrate and drink kool-aid after we're done, all the parents that is except Lew's and mine." He was referring to the fact that only his parents and mine hadn't made it to the graduation ceremony. Even Lyle's parents were there and he wasn't graduating.

He pushed the pot of matches towards Lyle and sat back down for the next hand. "So what's Ernie got in store for us?" The fight was over but he and Ernie still wouldn't look at each other.

I tossed the loose cards to Ernie and he shuffled them and started to deal.

"What's the kid gonna do after graduation?" Buddy was asking me.

"I dunno, fer sure," I said. "Ernie and I may be workin' out north along the river for awhile. That stretch up there is gonna be fenced so we gotta clear the cows off and get them to their home ranches."

"The cows got a home, but we got no homes," Buddy said. "Once you graduate, you can't hang with yer parents any more. You're on yer own. You ain't got no home. Now it don't matter to Ernie here cuz he's got no home anyway. His parents farmed him out so he's been on his own since he's a kid. But the rest of us had homes 'til today."

I didn't like the way he was still digging at Ernie. "It looks like Ernie wuz the lucky one then," I said. "He's been on his own a long time 'n now we gotta learn how."

"You-all gotta learn how," Buddy said with a smirk. "I'm gonna be in the army 'n the army takes care of its own."

"Sure, it does," I said. "My dad was in the army and he says it's the biggest fuckin' mess you ever did see."

"So whatcha gonna do after this summer," Buddy persisted, still looking at me. "You might as well join the army with me. The army's better than no home at all."

"I might try to get a job and go on to high school," I said. It was the first time I had said it out loud to anyone.

"Hah, fat chance o' that," Buddy scoffed. "Your old man hates school as much as my old man does. He ain't gonna send you to no high school."

"Just like you said, he ain't gonna send me, but that don't mean I can't go on my own," I said. I tossed two cards into the discard pile. I held back three deuces. I felt good about the hand I had this time.

Chapter 2

HOMEWARD

"Shit, I wish I hadn't joined the army," Buddy said.

Graduation was over, and we were hovering out of the snow in the hay shed behind the school. We had tossed our horses a scoop of oats and were waiting for them to finish eating before we saddled up and started home.

"So, some friend," I said, "you were tryin' to get me to join with you and now you say you wished you hadn't joined."

"I just wanted to get the hell outa here, and the army seemed to be the fastest way." He leaned back against a bale of hay. "Hell, even if you joined with me, we probably wouldn't go to the same place anyway. They just ship you any damn place they want to. You don't get to stay with yer friends."

"Who the hell said we were friends," I said, punching his arm, trying to cheer him up.

"Shit, this may be the last time I see you before I leave so don't give me a ration of shit. I leave for basic training next week."

"Jeez," I said, "I didn't know you left that soon.... But you'll do fine. My dad says basic is just a bunch of crap but nothing really had...except the tear gas. My dad said that was a bitch."

Mrs. Swift came around the corner of the school, her overshoes squeaking through the new snow. "Buddy, Lew," she called, "Where are you boys?"

"Right here," I yelled at her.

She slogged over to the hay lean-to, limping slightly on her right leg that had been injured in an accident when she was a teenager. Her leg now appeared thin and shrunken. She always wore heavy stocking to conceal the appearance of her leg, and she often used a cane to walk when, as she said, her leg was "bothering her." "Maybe, you boys shouldn't leave tonight," she panted, trying to get her breath from the exertion of walking through the new snow. "It's been warm all day, but it's down below freezing now, and it looks like a storm moving in. Maybe, you boys should stay in the cloakroom and ride home tomorrow in daylight." She leaned down so she could see under the roof of the hay shed. "I'll fix something to eat if you boys want to stay overnight."

"Naw, we'll be fine," Buddy said. "It ain't that far home."

"'Isn't,' Buddy," she answered, "'isn't that far home,' not 'ain't'."

"All right, ma'am." Buddy knew it made her angry to call her 'ma'am.'

"Mrs. Swift, please," she said. "It's not you I'm worried about so much anyway, Buddy. You don't have too far to go, but Lew has to cut through the badlands and cross the river. He won't get to the river 'til after dark now, and he could have trouble finding the crossing. Besides the ice could be breaking up, and he wouldn't be able to cross the river, especially if it's been melting and running off too much."

"I'll be okay, Mrs. Swift," I told her. Now that school was over, I didn't feel like camping overnight at the school house.

"Okay, but you boys come and tell me when you're leaving… and say goodbye. You're my two favorite pupils." She straightened up and walked back around the corner of the school, her cane leaving a small round hole in the crust of the snow.

"Her favorite pupils, my ass!" Buddy said. "I never could stand the old bitch. I just wish she'd take a hike."

"She's not so bad," I said. "The last time I had to stay over at school, she fixed a really good supper. She even made some cinnamon rolls for breakfast."

"Whoa," Buddy chortled, "you had breakfast with the old battle-axe, did you. She must have the hots for you. She sounded a lot more worried about you than about me."

"Hah, no way," I said.

"I don't know," Buddy went on teasingly. "She lives out here all alone by herself. I never seen her with no boy friend. And she's got that gimpy leg. She's probably hot for a piece of your tender young ass."

"Bull shit on you," I said. "I'm gonna saddle up." I crawled out from the hay lean-to and went to the horse barn. Old Yellow Dab, my big buckskin gelding, was lapping the last of his oats out of the grain box, so I left him alone. Buddy's little pinto whinnied longingly. He had finished his grain already and wanted more. I tossed a little more oats into his grain box, and he lapped it up with his large lips.

"Wow, what a softy you are," Buddy said at the door. "You'd never make a soldier anyway. Shit, a soldier has to be a hardass. You have to learn to be mean." He slapped his pinto on the croup but she ignored him.

"So she seems to know what kind of hardass you are," I said.

"We'll see about that," Buddy said. He picked up his bridle and walked into the stall. He jerked the little pinto's head out of her oats and stuck the bit into her mouth. She laid her ears back and tried to nip his arm. He stepped back and she went on eating her oats with the bit in her mouth. He tossed the blanket and saddle onto her back and tightened up the cinch. "So now who's boss?" he said, picking the last of the oats out of the grain box to feed her by hand.

"She sure found out what a mean hardass you are," I said jokingly. "Give her some more oats and she'll really get the picture."

He rubbed behind her ear and she nuzzled her muzzle against his chest. "Shit, you're the only thing I'm gonna miss around here," he said, scooping a little more oats so she could lap it from his hand.

"I thought you said you'd miss me," I said, slipping the bit into Yellow Dab's mouth.

"Not you or that big ugly buckskin you ride," he said. He backed his pinto out of her stall and led her to the door.

"Aren't you gonna tell Mrs. Swift you're leaving," I asked.

"Hell, no, let the old bitch whistle. Besides you're the one she's got the hots for. She don't want to see me." He led his pinto outside, but turned back to watch me tighten my cinch around Yellow Dab.

"Well, squirt, take care of yourself," he said. "I'll look you up when I get back from basic training." He held out his hand and we shook hands at the door. He mounted the little pinto and waved as he rode away.

I finished saddling Yellow Dab but left him in the stall with a little more oats. I slogged through the falling snow to the front of the school house.

Chapter 3

GOODBYES

Mrs. Swift was reading tests at her large oaken desk at the front of the classroom when I went in to say goodbye.

"Your test in history is the very best one in the class," she said when she looked up and saw me. "You really need to think about finishing high school and going on to college. Have you talked to your parents about going like I suggested you do?"

I avoided the question because I hadn't talked to them, and I knew my father was against the prospect of any further schooling. "My mother wants me to go on to high school in Bull Hook, I guess," I said.

"You could go to high school and right on the college in Bull Hook if you wanted to. You know North Montana Normal and Technical College is right there in Bull Hook. I'm sure you could do well enough in high school to get a scholarship to college."

"Yah, maybe," I said. The idea of college was so remote and unlikely that I hadn't even considered the prospect.

"So is Buddy still saddling up?" she asked.

"Nah," I said, "he already headed out fer home."

"Oh, that boy," Mrs. Swift said fretfully. "He always thinks he knows better what to do with his life than anyone else. I hope you're not planning to join the army also." She looked over her narrow reading glasses inquiringly.

"Nah," I said again. "My mom is really against that, so I guess I won't."

"Don't you let Buddy talk you into it now," she said, looking intently over her glasses at me.

"Well, I was sorta interested...but my mom's against it," I added again.

"You listen to your mom...and to me then. You belong in school, not in the army. Not right away anyway. There's plenty of time for that later after you finish college. Besides you're not old enough. I don't think they'd take you...even if you lied about your age." She paused a moment. "Like Buddy did," she added.

"Buddy lied about his age!!??" I said in total shock. "How could he do that?"

"He just added a few years to his age on his enlistment papers," she said. "The army recruiter wrote me a letter is how I know." She paused and stared at me disapprovingly. "But I wouldn't lie for you. So you're out of luck. Buddy's a few years older than you. And you don't look old enough, anyway. The recruiter would never believe you if you lied to him about your age."

"I wouldn't lie about my age," I said firmly, still reeling at the thought that Buddy had lied to the army. I wanted to ask if he would get into real trouble, but the thought was so disturbing I didn't even want to consider it.

"What will happen to him?" I asked hesitatingly.

"Oh, they'll probably take him all right unless someone volunteers the truth about his age. The recruiter's letter said he had gotten Buddy accepted into a sign-painting school in Honolulu. I figured that would be good training for Buddy. That's why I didn't say anything about his age." She sat back in her chair and looked at me intently.

"So you're determined to start home tonight, are you?" She went on. "I still wish you'd reconsider. It's been thawing the last couple of days. The river is liable to be too high for you to cross, so you might have to ride back and stay at the school anyway. Your dad left me strict orders for you to stay here if it's storming or if there's too much ice or too much run-off."

"But school's over now, so I should get on home," I said. I couldn't help a note of sorrow in my voice.

"So you like school all right, do you?" She reached for her cane and used it to lift herself to her feet.

"Yah, I'll miss it a little," I said, realizing for the first time that I actually would miss school. "It's okay most of the time," I added with a smile so she wouldn't take my genuine expression of feeling too seriously.

"You're a good boy," she said. She had moved so she was standing directly in front of me. She put her arms on my shoulders and drew me into an embrace. I felt her breasts push against my chest and detected a faint odor of lilac from her hair. I stood awkwardly with my arms at my sides while she held me against her for a minute, her head tucked under my chin.

"You're taller than I realized," she said, stepping back but holding me by the shoulders.

She looked at me directly in the face and I couldn't help looking back at her. We stood together staring at each other for another moment.

"I still think you shouldn't try to go home tonight," she said, "but I suppose you're determined. You be careful crossing that grade across the coulee down the county road there. There will probably be plenty of run-off there, too, after the last couple of days of thawing weather." She stepped back and walked behind her desk to her chair.

I felt somewhat relieved but a little unsettled—and aroused

also. I hadn't ever been hugged by a woman before except my aunt and grandmother. My mother was always very stand-offish about embracing her children. A little tap of affection on the shoulder was the most I was used to. I shuffled my feet uneasily.

"If the water is running over the road there at the culvert in the coulee, you come back here and stay at the school. Your father would never forgive me if I let you get into trouble on the road home," she said firmly, speaking now with authority in her large desk chair. The chair made her look even smaller than when she had been standing under my chin.

"I'll be okay," I said, turning to leave. At the door I turned back impulsively, "Thank you for being so nice," I said. I hesitated. "I'll try to go to high school," I added.

"Goodbye, Lew, and good luck," she said. "I know you'll be a big success in life."

"You're really very pretty," I said, "and not at all old." I couldn't stop the words that seemed to burst from my mouth with no conscious decision on my part. "And your leg doesn't matter a bit," I added, rushing through the door and running back to the horse barn before she could follow.

I hurried Yellow Dab out of his stall and galloped the first quarter mile down the county road heading home.

Chapter 4

ON THE ROAD

Yellow Dab was a tall horse with a long, rangy stride. I held him to a trot but we moved quickly going east down the county road. The sun was setting in the west, but the crimson streaks reflected off the snow crystals in the air and lit up the entire evening sky with a blushing pink haze. The sunset was so spectacular that I pulled Yellow Dab up for a moment to look at the western sky. The sun was a fireball of crimson hovering just above the horizon in the southwestern sky. The snow covering the ground and the snow falling both reflected pink halos across the wide flat horizon to the west. For a moment, I felt that I should offer a prayer, even though I had long since given up the consoling thought that God was really alive.

Yellow Dab shook his head impatiently. The sunset didn't have the same sacred appeal for him. I let him resume his rapid pace down the narrow country road. I wondered if horses regarded their human masters in somewhat the same way as their masters regarded God. They know us too well, I thought with a smile. Humans attribute all sorts of powers and virtues to God without fear of contradiction because no one knows what God is like. But horses know the fallibility of their human masters only too well.

Suddenly, Yellow Dab stopped dead in the middle of the road with his ears cocked forward. In the sudden silence I could hear it, too. Running water! We were near the coulee that cut across the road and I could hear the gush of running water.

"That has to be too much water to be running through the culvert," I said aloud to Yellow Dab. "It must be running over the road."

I urged Yellow Dab forward until we could look down into the coulee bed. The road was graded about fifteen feet above the stream bed and, usually the stream flow went through a culvert. Now, the water flow was far too heavy for the culvert. Two or three feet of water were flowing over the road.

The water on the downstream side of the grade was also unusually deep. On the downstream side it was falling only a little over four feet, so the water itself in the stream below the grade had to be over ten feet deep.

Yellow Dab didn't want to approach the stream at all. He tried to bow his neck to the side and turn away. I used the reins to jerk his head back again towards the stream and kicked him forward. He wasn't used to my sharp treatment so he moved ahead in a series of quick jumps.

I stopped him just at the edge of the running water and patted his neck. I didn't want him to throw a fit after we got into the water.

"It's okay, boy," I said. I patted his neck repeatedly with a gentle stroke and leaned forward to speak softly close above his ears. "If we stay on the road, boy, we'll be fine. See there. The water's only a coupla feet deep. No big deal. We stay on the road and we make it across. No problem. I don't even get my feet wet and you'll be just fine. We'll be home in no time."

Even as I said we'd be fine, I was thinking ahead about the river. "Christ," I said aloud to myself. "If the river's breaking up like this coulee, we'll never get across that."

I leaned forward to speak to Yellow Dab again. "There's only one way to see what the river's doing. That's ride down there and take a look. We gotta go, boy."

"Oh, my God," I spoke to myself again. "We can't even try to cross the river if the ice is near breaking up. Dad, you've told me a hundred times at least. You can't cross the river on the ice if you think there's any chance it may break up. You could be sucked under the ice by the current even on horseback. And then you're a goner."

"We gotta go look at it." I leaned forward and spoke reassuringly to Yellow Dab again. Even I knew I was trying to reassure myself as much as I was trying to calm him down.

"Enough of this bull shit," I spoke louder than I intended and Yellow Dab took a hopping step into the stream.

"Good boy," I said patting his neck as we edged forward. "Just stay upstream on the road grade and we'll be fine."

And we might have been, "but the luck of the draw wasn't with us" was how I told the story to Buddy later on.

Yellow Dab was in a hurry to get across and out of the freezing water. I held the reins very taut so he couldn't lower his head, but he still tried to lunge ahead anyway, jerking desperately at the reins. Suddenly, I felt his back give way under me and I had to grab the horn to keep my seat in the saddle. I lost my grip on the reins and my head snapped back at the same time as I felt Yellow Dab falling forward under me. The road under us seemed to melt into the rushing water, and the sudden freezing gush of water swept us uncontrollably downstream.

"Oh, Christ, it washed out," was the last thing I could remember saying to Yellow Dab as we were immersed in the icy water cascading downstream from the roadbed.

Yellow Dab was a strong swimmer and he hit the rushing current with a lunging struggle towards the opposite bank. I didn't dare get off his back to help swim because I was afraid I'd lose him in the strong current of the stream. I headed him downstream so he wouldn't have to struggle so hard against the rushing water.

Once he felt the current push him along, he swam strongly to the shore and struggled his way up the icy bank.

"Good boy, good boy," I said patting his sopping wet neck. I could already feel ice crystals forming in his hair.

When I felt the ice on his neck, I also realized that my own pants were beginning to freeze stiff. "I've got to walk a ways," I said to myself, "or I'll freeze my ass off for sure."

I stepped stiffly off Yellow Dab's back. My boots sloshed water as they hit the ground. "Christ, they feel like two buckets of ice water," I said quietly to Yellow Dab, patting his neck.

"We've gotta get going," I added, starting to lead him down the road once again. I walked beside him so I could continue talking to him. "Dad always says if you're stuck in winter you gotta keep moving," I continued. "You can't stop, no matter how tired you get. To stop is to freeze. And to freeze is to die."

I could hear my dad's harsh voice giving me instructions as we trudged through the newly fallen snow.

"Here's the gate we gotta go through," I said to Yellow Dab, as I opened the wire gate." I couldn't get my freezing hands to work to close the gate so I left it lying open. I could hear my dad's reproving voice. "If you go through a gate that's closed, you close it when you get through. You never leave it open…never."

"We'll come back and close it later," I spoke quietly to Yellow Dab. "We gotta cross this field and find the trail through the badlands that goes down to the riverbed. God, dark as it is, we'll have a hell of a time finding that trail. But we'll just have to hit the edge of the badlands and scout along them until we hit the trail."

"God," I thought, "which way do we go when we hit the badlands, upriver or downriver, left or right?"

"There's no goddam way we'll know for sure which way the trail is when we hit the badlands," I whispered to Yellow Dab. "We'll just have to range up and back until we find it." I could feel my voice was going. I started to whisper to Yellow Dab but I couldn't form a sound. The sudden silence was eery. I tried to form words and could not.

Suddenly, I felt I was no longer walking. I felt I was floating high above the ground moving effortlessly forward. I could look down and see myself and Yellow Dab struggling through the snow banks. Ahead from my vantage point high above I could see the badlands. "God, we're just about there," I thought to myself because I could no longer speak.

Suddenly I realized I could no longer hear either. The crunching of the footfalls in the snow had disappeared. I looked down at myself far below and forced myself to take another step forward.

It was no use. I had hit a wall and could no longer go forward. I forced my hand out and felt ahead. At first, I was puzzled by what I was touching, but then I realized it was the flank of a horse.

"Is that you, Yellow Dab?" I forced myself to say, and suddenly I heard the sound of my own voice. Equally as suddenly, I was wide awake and alert.

"Jesus Christ, I must have been asleep and dreaming," I said to myself. "Walking in my sleep. Good boy, Old Yellow, you were dragging me along to keep me from freezing and when you stopped I walked into your rear end."

"Good boy, good boy," I kept repeating quietly to Yellow Dab. "Christ, while I was asleep, you kept me walking." I forced myself to step forward and pat him on the neck. "Good boy, good boy," I repeated.

I leaned my head against Yellow Dab's neck for a moment. He turned his head and nuzzled my chest with his nose. I forced myself to take another step ahead of him and brushed the snow out of my eyes.

I looked in amazement. "And, my God," I almost shouted. "You knew where we were going and you led us right to the trail."

I rubbed my eyes again. There was only a faint glow from the sunset, but I could plainly see the cow trail or old buffalo trail—that snaked around the side of a gumbo butte and led to the river bottom below.

My feet were so cold I could no longer feel them, but I moved forward with a new burst of energy, leading Yellow Dab down the side of the butte. At the bottom the trail led through a cottonwood grove containing patches of buck brush and wild rose bushes, all leafless and pushing their stiff stems through the snow cover.

"We gotta stop, old boy, and see if we can warm up," I told Yellow Dab. He nuzzled my back as I kicked a hole in the snow and enlarged it into a small circle. I had stopped by a fallen cottonwood and gathered dead branches and any larger chunks of wood I could find.

With my pocketknife I shaved off slivers from a dried limb until I had a small pile of shavings in the middle of the clearing I had created.

"Oh, Christ," I whispered to Yellow Dab, "I hope the matches didn't get wet." I reached into the left saddle bag behind my saddle and felt around for the small can that contained matches.

"Jesus, they're still dry," I said to Yellow Dab, as I extracted a couple of matches from the can. I flicked a match with my fingernail and it burst into flame with a bright snap. I touched it to the pile of shavings and they quickly caught fire.

"Christ, that was a lot easier than in Jack London's story," I said to Yellow Dab. "Now, we have to watch out for a falling bank of snow," I added, recalling the events in Jack London's story. In his story the fire his character has such trouble getting started is doused by a bank of snow falling from an overhead branch. And then the character's dog abandons him and he gives up and freezes to death.

"No overhead branches, old boy," I said to Yellow Dab gleefully, "and besides you're a horse, not a damn dog. Horses are a helluva lot better than dogs." I patted Yellow Dab's neck. "And horses like you are a helluva lot smarter and more loyal than dogs," I added. "And we ain't gonna give up either, by God!" I didn't believe that what I said was necessarily true, but I was feeling lightheaded and felt I had to say something encouraging that would buck up Yellow Dab's spirits.

I added bigger branches to the fire and it hissed away melting a wider circle of snow. I sat on a branch of the downed tree and slowly slipped my boots and heavy wool socks off and hung them on a branch near the fire.

My toes were frozen, but I held them out to the fire and clutched them snugly between my bare hands. They began to itch and ache with excruciating pain.

"Christ, they must be thawing out, old boy," I said to Yellow Dab. "I hope I got them thawed out in time so I don't get gangrene or something."

Yellow Dab nuzzled my shoulder insistently.

"Calm down, old boy," I said, "I'll get you a taste of oats when my damn socks and boots thaw out enough to put back on."

He didn't seem to mind the delay. He was enjoying the fire as much as I was.

Chapter 5

THE RIVER

I drowsed by the fire for a couple of hours while my boots and socks dried and while I thawed my feet. Yellow Dab hung his head and seemed to drowse by the side of the fire also.

After my shoes and socks dried, I was running out of the dry branches that thrust up through the snow enough to provide good fuel. My feet were still hurting like hell, but I decided I'd better get ready to move. The half-moon was now showing enough through the gently drifting snow that I would be better able to see where I was going.

I pulled the socks on gently, but the pain from my feet brought tears to my eyes. Then I had to tackle my boots. I was afraid my feet had swollen, so I decided I would have to pull the boots on with one quick tug.

I positioned the boot with my foot inserted as far as it would go without effort. Then, I offered a mighty jerk on the boot straps.

I exhaled a short scream of pain and Yellow Dab looked at me quizzically.

"Son-of-a-bitch," I said. "It's still not clear on. My feet must be really swollen.

I braced myself, took a deep breath, and jerked the boot on with one more effort.

"Jesus Christ," I moaned to Yellow Dab. "Now, we still gotta go with boot two."

But boot two was easier. I knew what to expect, so I simply jerked it on and ignored the pain. I dug a handful of oats out of my other saddle bag and held it out to Yellow Dab, who scarfed it up eagerly. I kicked my feet on the ground and moved around in my little clearing to get my circulation up.

"Well, let's get going," I told Yellow Dab. I tightened the cinch I had loosened and swung stiffly into the saddle. I figured I'd give my sore feet a break by riding for a ways until I got too cold.

I skirted the cottonwood grove until I found the path that would take us to the bank of Milk 'n Honey River. The world was full of quiet shadows as I rode through the cottonwood grove. The bare limbs of the cottonwoods flitted in front of the moon and made it appear to be smiling.

I wasn't far into the grove before I could hear the ice grinding in the river. It sounded like breaking glass.

"God, that doesn't sound too damn good," I said to Yellow Dab, patting his neck.

I could feel the tension in his withers as he heard the sound of the ice. "You probably think I'm dumb enough to jump you into the river to swim through that ice," I said to him with what I hoped would be a reassuring ring in my voice. "But I'm not that dumb."

When we drew near the edge of the cottonwood grove, I could see the river had risen until it was flowing bank full. From shore to shore, the entire channel was full of large ice floes, softly grinding together as they rushed downstream.

I paused for a minute, looking at the line of light from the moon reflecting off the water between the chunks of ice. Most of the ice floes were still covered with snow, so I knew the river was just beginning to break up. A few days before, it had been solid ice from shore to shore with drifted snow making shadowy patterns across the bare surface. The scene of the gently flowing river seemed utterly serene and consoling, but I knew there was no chance for us to get across.

"No way through that goddam mess," I said to Yellow Dab, patting his neck so he'd calm down. Even through the saddle, I could feel his withers quivering as he eyed the river. Each time the ice floes made a particularly shrill grinding sound, he tried to edge a little farther back from the bank. When I held him facing the river, he laid his ears back in disapproval.

"Easy, boy," I said to him quietly, "even I'm not crazy enough to tackle that mess tonight." He seemed to understand my meaning because I could feel his withers gradually relax, and his ears snapped forward.

"Well, hell," I said to him, turning his head away from the river. "We can't go back across that damn flooded coulee, so we better head upriver. We can probably make it far enough up to skirt that coulee and get back to the school." I stopped myself from thinking about what I would do when I got back to the school.

I patted Yellow Dab's neck as we headed back up the trail through the woods. His quickened gait reflected his definite approval of my decision to go back.

When we reached the edge of the woods, we headed upriver at a fast walk. My feet were beginning to feel cold again, so I figured I'd better walk a ways.

"Your feet freeze lots easier after they've just been frozen," I told Yellow Dab. "I guess it has to do with constricted blood vessels."

When I stepped out of the saddle to walk, he nudged me approvingly. He was getting tired, too.

We crossed a meadow along the river where wheat-grass heads

were waving above the snow. I stopped and let Yellow Dab crop a few. I no longer felt the same urgency I'd felt earlier. The decision was now made. I had no more choices in what I had to do. "Our best shot is to take our time and get our asses back to the school," I told Yellow Dab.

"You must think I'm a real wimp," I went on, patting his neck as he calmly munched a mouthful of wheat-grass. "First, I'm in a helluva sweat to get down the road away from school. Then, I can't wait to get back."

I patted his neck and rubbed between his ears when he put his head down to get another mouthful of grass. "It's stuff like that, that makes you horses know we're not gods," I patted his neck.

"Well, grab another mouthful and let's get going," I told him. I let him crop another mouthful of wheatgrass heads, then urged him on across the field.

When we got to the edge of the field, the ridge line we were on dropped off, and the field ahead was running a full width of water as far as I could see.

"Damn," I told Yellow Dab, "I wish the damn moon were a little farther west and we could probably see how wide this damn stream is."

I paused a minute and patted his neck again. "Well, it's probably not gonna be very wide across, but I ain't wading all the way. You're gonna have to let me ride across on your back."

I crawled stiffly aboard the saddle, the pain from my feet almost causing me to cry out once more. "I don't think they're frozen up again, anyway," I said to Yellow Dab. I wiggled the toes in both of my boots. Both feet hurt excruciatingly with even the slightest movement.

I kicked Yellow Dab forward into the running stream. It was

mostly a result of newly melted snow so there were only a few small ice chunks bobbing their way downstream. The stream-bed we were crossing was only a couple of feet deep, but it seemed to stretch an endless distance before we went up a small rise and into another cottonwood grove.

I wasn't as familiar with this grove, so I skirted it as much as I could while staying above the stream of winter run-off. I circled the grove to the south towards the badlands and finally spotted an animal trail that was well-worn enough to appear as if it should lead through the cottonwoods and underbrush.

I stopped Yellow Dab and dismounted slowly. My feet were hurting like fury, but I was getting drowsy and cold so I needed to walk.

The path through the cottonwood grove wound back and forth skirting stands of buck brush and buffalo-berry bushes. The moon was nearly straight overhead now, and I felt a kind of bliss at the serene walk through the grove, even forgetting the agony of my swollen, aching feet.

When I reached the edge of the woods, I spotted a light across the plowed field that was on the far side of the cottonwoods. It looked like someone must live along the river valley, but I couldn't think for a moment who it could be.

"Jesus," I said to Yellow Dab, "we must have come a long ways farther than I thought. This must be the DuMont place." The DuMonts were Ernie's foster parents, and they also had a daughter named Anne Marie, who was in the fifth grade at the Burnham School.

"I'll be damned," I said again to Yellow Dab. "We must have come a helluva lot farther than I realized." From DuMont's place there was a graded road that went up through the badlands and then met the same county road that I had taken when I left the Burnham School hours earlier. The difference was that the road from DuMont's met the county road about a mile and a half west of the school, and we had taken the same road from the school over a mile and a half east before we had cut across the field leading north to the badlands along the river. "Jesus, boy, we made a helluva lot of miles since we took off," I whispered in Yellow Dab's ear.

There was a light on in the barn at the DuMont place, but I couldn't decide if I wanted to stop or not.

Chapter 6

NEW BIRTH

I couldn't stay undecided about stopping at the DuMonts for long. Yellow Dab made up my mind for me. He sensed or smelled a barn with hay and grain and who knows what other luxuries. He began to walk briskly towards the lighted barn and I let him go.

There was a corral in front of the lighted door of the barn. I could barely manage to get the gate open. I opened it enough to usher Yellow Dab through and he snapped around smartly so I could push the gate shut and latch it. Luckily, it had an automatic latch, so I didn't have to fumble at it with my stiffened fingers.

I led Yellow Dab towards the lighted barndoor, where I could hear what clearly appeared to be the sounds of human activity. Ernie came through the door just before I reached it. Speechlessly, he stared at me for a moment with a pallid expression and then he turned quickly and vomited against the side of the barn.

"Christ, what's wrong?" I said. "Are you sick or something? What the hell is wrong?"

"Jesus Christ, there's a goddam ewe in there that's got a goddam lamb stuck in her belly," Ernie said, "Christ, we've been tryna git it out for an hour, but no goddam luck. It's stuck too goddam tight. I couldn't take it any more. I had to get out and throw my guts up."

"Come on, you chickenshit town kid," I said. "I've been delivering lambs with my old man since before I could walk. Let's get back in there and get that lamb out. What kind of midwife are you?"

"Hell, no," he backed up and put his hands up as if he were trying to hold me off. "I ain't goin' back in there. Christ's own horses couldn't drag me back."

"Jesus Christ," I answered impatiently. "Just show me where the goddam sheep is and I'll drag that little son-of-a-bitchin' lamb out by myself."

"Listen, the old man, Lucien, is in there now. He doesn't know shit about delivering lambs, but maybe he can give you a hand or you can give him a hand. I'm just gonna sit here and let you two miracle-workers do your thing."

"Have it your way, lily liver," I said, punching his arm. He pushed me into the barn and sat down in the doorway with his back to me.

I walked into the small clapboard sheep barn and headed towards the stall in back that I could see was lighted with a big kerosene lantern. A small dark complected Metis man, Lucien DuMont, had his back leaning against one of the two-by-fours that supported the dividers between the stalls.

"Hey, Lucien," I said, "Ernie tells me you're having trouble getting a lamb out."

"Huh!" Lucien said, "Christ, you startled me. I thought you were Ernie coming back."

"Naw, Ernie's outside throwing his guts up."

"God, I don't blame him," Lucien said with a painful note of discouragement in his voice. "Christ, I can't do anything with this son-of-bitch. We've tried half the night to get that goddam lamb out but nothin' doin'. We're gettin' nowhere. I'm afraid we're gonna kill both the ewe and the lamb if we don't get something done soon."

"Well, that could happen all right," I said, "Young ewes like this are kind of delicate when they deliver their first lamb.

Sometimes they both just die and there isn't a damn thing you or God can do about it. These young ewes don't have very big openings between their pelvic bones, and sometimes their lambs are so big they won't fit through."

I paused a minute. I didn't want to make him feel like I was butting into his business.

"I could take a look if you don't mind," I said with cautious diffidence.

"Hell, yes, be my guest," he shrugged. "You couldn't possibly screw it up worse than we already have. I'm gonna go catch a breather for a minute. Help yourself. Just call me if you need me."

"Naw, I won't need any help for a minute," I said, relieved that he hadn't taken offense at my cutting in. "But I could use some iodine or antiseptic sheep-dip if you got some handy," I asked him as he turned to leave.

"Christ, I never even thought of using it. There's a dishpan of water and some soap and a rag over there, though." He pointed to the far side of the stall. "I s'pose the water's gittin' pretty cold but you can wash off if you want."

He looked so defeated as he turned and walked towards the door that I didn't interrupt him again.

I looked down at the ewe for a minute. I was so tired my eyes weren't focusing very well, but I could readily see she wasn't going to make it much longer.

"Shit, goddam halfassed amateurs," I said, grinning to myself at my arrogant, know-it-all tone. "Christ, they should have got this handled a helluva lot faster and then the ewe and lamb both would have a helluva lot better chance." I was determined to do my best to deliver the lamb now. It became a matter of principle. If I was going to be so arrogant, I'd better be able to prove I had the goods.

33

"Shit, I've delivered a hundred lambs at least," I said to myself, as I took off my shirt and scrubbed my hands and arms in the lukewarm water."

"Christ, my hands are stiff as boards," I said. "Maybe I froze them a little bit, too."

"Shit, they hurt like hell," I thought to myself. I didn't want to admit that out loud.

The ewe had her front legs tied together with the rope looped around one of the two-by-fours dividing the stalls. She was lying on her side and her lower back leg was tied to the opposite side of the stall.

"Well, Christ, at least they did that right," I said aloud to myself again.

I kneeled down behind the ewe. I clenched my stiff right hand together forming as small a ball as I could with my fingers extended and clamped into as narrow a point as I could make.

I slipped my wet hand into the ewe's womb and felt the lamb's nose with the tips of my fingers. I expanded my fingers so I could feel the size of the lamb's head.

"Christ almighty," I almost felt like crying. "That goddam lamb's head is never going to fit between those pelvic bones. Jesus Christ!"

I stood up. Now, I felt as discouraged as Lucien had sounded. I washed my hands off carefully again and dried them on the rag lying beside the dishpan.

I walked towards the barn door and spotted both Ernie and Lucien standing just inside the door passing a cigarette back-and-forth between them. "Want a cigarette, kid," Lucien asked. He shook his pack of tailor-mades so a cigarette stuck above the pack. He held it towards me.

"Nah, thanks," I said shyly.

"Shit, Big Lew doesn't smoke or drink, either one," Ernie said. "He's fuckin' pure as the driven snow."

"Nah, he's just too damn young to drink or smoke," Lucien said kindly. "Well, kid, what did you find out with that damn little ewe? By Christ, I'm about to give up on the pair of 'em. I'm never gonna raise fuckin' sheep again. The sons-of-bitches will fall over and die if a heavy breeze hits 'em." He ground the cigarette into the dry manure of the corral with the toe of his boot.

"Well, it's looking pretty damn bad," I said. "The ewe is damn weak, and the lamb may already be dead." I paused for a moment to get my thinking together. I was feeling vague and light-headed from cold and exhaustion.

"We can go two ways," I continued. "The lamb's head is absolutely too big to go past the mother's pelvic bones. If we figure the lamb's dead for sure, we can go in and crush his head and try to get it past the pelvic bones that way; then we can loop a rope over his front legs and pull the rest of him out."

I paused and stomped my feet on the manure of the corral to try to warm them up. They were hurting so bad I could barely keep from crying out loud.

"What's the other way?" Lucien asked. "You said there were two possible ways." I was pleased he appeared to be deferring to me as the expert—whether I was really expert or not. Actually, I wasn't expert at all with either of the two ways, but I'd helped my dad deliver so many lambs I figured I had a shot at trying either approach.

"The other way is, we could do a caesarian section," I said, trying to get a ring of sincerity and authority into my voice. "That way, you shave the ewe's belly and clean it off and disinfect it and then you cut in and deliver the lamb through the belly. Then, we gotta sew the ewe up and that's it. If we were sure the lamb was still alive, that would be the way to go." Despite my fatigue I was feeling more alert at the prospect we might try a caesarian. I had never really done one, but I had watched my dad work on delivering both calves and lambs that way, and I had always wanted to give it a try for myself.

"Well, Jesus," Lucien said, "that sounds a helluva lot better to me but shit if I know." He shook out another cigarette and scratched a match up his pant leg. He took a couple of deep puffs, then passed the cigarette to Ernie. Apparently, they were used to sharing cigarettes. "Which the hell way would you go?" he finally asked.

"I think I'd go caesarian. It's a long shot and the lamb's probably dead already. And the ewe will probably die, too, because she's getting real weak. This has been going on too long for her to be in very good shape. But it's a double damn cinch they'll both die if we don't do something." For the first time, I wished I were a smoker so I could ask for a drag on the Camel they were passing back and forth. "And damn fast, too," I added firmly, "that poor ewe ain't gonna last much longer."

"Well, shit, let's git to it then," Lucien said. "What kinda tools do you need to do the job? Let's go up to the house and round up what you need."

We started for the house. "Mainly, we need a good safety razor with a couple of extra blades, some more hot water and soap, some iodine or sheep dip if you got any, and a big needle with some very heavy thread to sew her up afterwards. But the main thing we need is a helluva sharp skinning knife or butcher knife to cut into her. And we need a whetstone to keep the blade sharp," I paused when we mounted the porch and went into the house. "In case we run into some trouble we need an extra lamp to heat a branding iron. And we need a bum lamb nursing bottle with a nipple," I added, as we stepped through the door into what was obviously the kitchen.

"What trouble could we possibly have?" Lucien said laughing. He went to the cupboard and plucked a beautiful skinning knife from a knife holder. The knife had a trim, elegant, curved blade and an ivory handle. He picked up a whetstone from the counter and held them both out to me.

"It's a pretty goddam special occasion when I let anybody use my skinning knife," he said. "But sharpen her up and I'll look for the other shit."

He started through the door into another room, then turned back for a moment. "And sit down, for Christ's sake, Ernie. You don't, for God's sake, have to watch if you don't feel up to it." He went through the door and we heard him strike a match and shuffle around looking for a needle and thread.

"If you don't feel up to what, Ernie?" said a young girl's voice from another direction. I looked up from where I was whetting the knife carefully back and forth on the whetstone, turning it over for each stroke so it would sharpen absolutely evenly on both sides of the blade.

I watched Anne Marie come into the room from her bedroom. I could see her bed behind her with the covers thrown back. She was wearing a white flannel nightgown. Her bare feet shown below the bottom hem of her heavy nightgown. They were elegantly thin and long with high arches. She was a shy pretty girl with a light brown complexion and black hair in two long tight Indian braids thrown forward over her shoulders. The braids were tied as I always saw them at school, with two large red ribbons and carefully fashioned knots with two large bows each.

We had never spoken to each other at school, but I had often admired her from a distance. I thought she was by far the best looking of the girls at Burnham School. There were seven girls ranging from the first to the fifth grade at the school. Anne Marie was the tallest of the group. She was not the oldest but she was in the highest grade and was clearly the best student among the girls in the lower grades.

"What the shit do you care?" Ernie said. "It's none of your business, baby girl." He was hanging his head, feeling ashamed and defensive about his squeamishness.

Anne Marie backed up against the wall and hung her head. I had planned to stay out of the conversation, but she looked so forlorn and upset I felt I had to say something to her.

"It's just a ewe that's trying to have a lamb," I said to her, "and she's having a little trouble, so we're going to have to give her some help."

When I spoke, she glanced around and saw me for the first time.

"Oh my goodness," she said, and darted back into her bedroom and shut the door. In a few short minutes, she came back out again. She had donned a pair of dark pants and a white blouse. I was disappointed to notice she had covered her elegant bare feet in furry bedroom slippers.

"I'm sorry," she said. "I had no idea there was anyone here other than Dad and what's his name, Mr. Smarty Pants, over there." She jerked her thumb in Ernie's direction. "And he doesn't count for anything," she added, sticking her tongue out at Ernie.

"So did you like our skit today?" I asked her. "Where we played the old farm ladies?"

"Yeah, it was really cute," she said gaily. "You were really very funny, but Mr. Stupid over there almost messed it up." She started to stick her tongue out at Ernie again but stopped herself. She seemed to grow from a smart-alecky little girl to a polite young woman in just that moment.

"May I get you a cup of coffee or tea?" she asked me. "I know we have lots of hot water on the stove so I can get you some instant coffee in just a second or we have some tea bags in the cupboard. Whichever you want?"

"I guess I better have some coffee," I said. "To wake myself up for the operation," I added with a polite smile.

"Oh, operation, what operation do you mean?" she asked. She took four coffee mugs out of the cupboard and lined them up on the counter. Carefully, she measured a large teaspoonful of instant Folger's into each cup.

"Oh, I just meant trying to deliver this lamb. It's probably going to be kind of a tough delivery," I said dismissively. I didn't want to make it sound like too big a deal.

"Oh, can I help?" she asked with an excited ring in her voice. "I love to help with the sheep. They're so cute and sweet. I know Daddy doesn't like them very much, but I just love them. I wish we'd get rid of the cows and just raise sheep and horses." She scooped hot water from the large oblong tub on the top of the kitchen stove and filled the four coffee cups. She gave each cup two quick stirs with a teaspoon.

Carefully, she picked up the first cup of coffee. "If you don't think I can help, can I just come out and watch? I think sheep are so interesting." She started her statement in the beseeching tones of a child, then caught herself and finished with a somewhat affected formality.

"As far as I'm concerned, you can watch or help, whatever," I said. "But you better ask your dad, and you're going to have to put on different shoes and a warm coat and hat. It's pretty cold out tonight. Spring's already over after just a few days."

She served one of the mugs of coffee to Ernie, who accepted the coffee but ignored her. Then, she grabbed up one of the other mugs and hurried towards her bedroom.

"Daddy will let me help," she said confidently. "He can't refuse me anything I really want," she added with a gay pirouette. "Oh, and tell him when he comes out that he has a cup of coffee on the counter," she finished excitedly and stuck out her tongue at Ernie as she disappeared into her bedroom and shut the door once more.

"Christ, we don't want that spoiled, dippy girl getting in the way out at the barn," Ernie said with a sour tone. "What a total dipshit she is anyway!"

"I don't give a damn either way," I said. "Maybe she'd be willing to help out a bit...." I continued and was going to add, "...since you're too much of a town boy sissy to watch," but I decided that would be rubbing it in too much. Ernie was already feeling bad enough about his squeamishness.

"Hell," Ernie whispered to me so neither Anne Marie nor her dad would overhear. "That mean little bitch gets her own way on everything. She just whines to her old man and he lets her do anything. Her mother ain't like that, though. Her mother's pretty tough on her."

I started to answer Ernie but I heard Lucien coming back.

"Well, I got some sheep dip, a big needle and heavy thread, and a couple of clean towels. You're gonna wear that blade out if you sharpen it any more. Let's get to it." Lucien's voice had taken on a new air of confidence and energy.

"Anne Marie made you a cup of coffee there," I said, nodding in the direction of the last mug of steaming coffee. I touched the blade of the skinning knife with my thumb. It felt sharp indeed.

"Oh, good" he said, setting his box of tools down and picking up the coffee. "I'm sorry we woke her up, but I guess it couldn't be helped. Anyway, school's over for the summer, so she can sleep in tomorrow if she wants to."

"Oh, she also wants to help with the sheep," I added on Anne Marie's behalf.

"Oh, she always wants to help with the sheep." There was feigned annoyance in his voice but also a touch of pride. He took a sip of his coffee. "I guess she's gonna turn out to be the sheepman in this family. Her mother sure hates sheep anyway…even more than I do."

I stood up and started to hand the knife and whetstone to Lucien. "No, you keep them," he said. "You appear to know more about what you're doing here than I do." He took a final sip of coffee and set his mug down.

"Hey, little girl," he added in a loud enough tone to be heard in Anne Marie's bedroom, "Hurry up! That poor ewe can't wait all night for you."

"'Ewe' can't wait for 'you'. Very cute, Daddy!" Anne Marie flitted across the room and kissed her dad on the cheek. "I'm glad you're gonna let me help out with the ewe's birthing problems. I'll help out the very best way I can."

"Ernie, grab a coupla buckets and fill 'em with hot water and bring 'em along," Lucien said to Ernie.

Then he turned to Anne Marie. "If your mother were here, you know she'd throw a fit about this, so don't you dare tell her when she gets back." As we started out the door, he turned to Anne

Marie again and added in a much more serious voice. "You know this ewe and lamb both are pretty likely gonna die. You gotta be prepared for that and not throw a fuss when it happens."

"I know, Daddy," Anne Marie answered gaily. "And you know I wouldn't think of being any problem to my sweet daddy."

Chapter 7

MIRACLES

"Jesus, kid," Lucien said to me quietly on the way to the barn, "you look tired as hell. I know you know how to deliver this lamb cuz I know you help your dad all the time. But are you sure yer up to this?"

"Yeah, I should be okay," I said. "I'm just a little tired is all."

"You and yer horse look like you hit the drink. I hope you didn't try crossin' the river with all that goddam ice."

"Nah," I told him, "the road washed out on that county road east of the school and we had to swim for it."

"Jeez, bad luck," he said. "Now, you can't cross the river either. You could stay here a few days if you need to, 'til the ice clears on the river."

"Nah," I said, "my dad pays a little so I can stay in the cloakroom at the school…on the cot there, if I can't make it home."

"Okay, kid," he said, "but yer welcome to stay here anytime."

"Thanks," I said, "but since my dad pays he'll expect me at the school, so he might come by to pick me up."

"Yeah, that's true," Lucien said. "He wouldn't know where the hell you were if he showed up and you weren't at school."

"Oh," I said, remembering we hadn't picked up an extra lamp, "we better have an extra lamp or two to heat the branding iron and for a little extra light."

"Hey, little girl," Lucien told Anne Marie, "run and get those two extra lamps on the kitchen table…and bring some more matches, too."

Anne Marie pirouetted about and saluted her father. "Yes, sir, daddy dear, but don't you do anything neat until I get back."

"Well, kid," Lucien said, "you still never told me what we need the hot branding iron for."

"If we hit a blood vessel or something when we cut in," I explained, "we can cauterize it with the hot iron…or if the bleeding gets too bad, the hot iron will sometimes stop it."

"'Sometimes' is right, I guess," Lucien said, "and if it don't stop the bleeding, it's goodbye, Mr. Sheep."

"That's about right," I said.

After we got to the sheep's stall, we laid out our tools on a shelf and I carefully trimmed the wool and tags—mats of dirty wool—from the ewe's belly. I then soaped up her belly and began to shave a long strip from her bag to her rib cage.

"You can try to get a little milk out of her bag into one of them nursing bottles," I told Lucien. "We may need some of that new mother's milk to get the lamb started if he can't nurse right away."

Lucien took the big nipple off one of the nursing bottles and tried to squeeze a little milk from the ewe's tit. His awkward efforts only produced a couple of drops.

"Here," I offered, "take over the shaving and I'll see what I can do with her."

"I ain't use tuh milkin' a damn sheep," he said as we exchanged places. I massaged the ewe's bag for a minute and then squirted several large streams of new milk from each of her tits. "She seems to have plenty of milk," I said. "If she lives, you won't have a bum lamb anyway. She should be able to nurse him okay."

Just as we finished the milking and shaving of the ewe, Anne

Marie brought two extra kerosene lamps into the stall and placed them on the shelf. "Wow, she really looks naked," she said pointing at the ewe's belly. "But I warned you not to start without me." She patted her father's head playfully where he had it still bent over the sheep's belly.

"Well, we would've waited," Lucien said, "but the patient's needs concerned us more than the nurse's whims." He stood up and looked proudly at the results of his shaving. "Where's that goddam Ernie gone off to now?" he asked looking around for Ernie.

"The pansy can't take it," Anne Marie answered.

"Well, I guess I did tell him he didn't have to stay if he didn't want to watch," Lucien conceded.

"You're too nice, sweet daddy," Anne Marie said. "He's just a no good lazy loafer and you know it."

"Go easy on Ernie now," Lucien said. "He's from town and there's a lot he don't know about ranching, but he works hard enough at jobs he can do."

"But he can't do anything at all," Anne Marie answered.

"You gotta paint her stomach with that sheep dip to disinfect it," I interrupted, looking on as he put the finishing touches to shaving the ewe's stomach. I was eager to get going with the actual incision. The longer it took to get started, the more my stomach had time to feel queasy and nervous.

I kneeled beside the ewe with the ivory handled skinning knife cradled lightly in my hand. "You better hold her upper leg so she can't kick around," I said to Lucien. "And can you bring me the hot branding iron if I need it?" I asked Anne Marie.

"As you wish, Dr. Lew," she said gaily. It was the first time she'd ever called me by my name. I smiled at her. Her good spirits brought a sense of confidence to my preparations.

I cut a neat gash in the ewe's belly with the sharp blade of the skinning knife sliding easily through the flesh of ewe's stomach. She bleated mournfully and tried to struggle out of Lucien's firm grasp. I asked for the hot iron and gently cauterized several places where it was bleeding most heavily, causing the poor ewe to bleat even louder.

After I wiped the blood from her gaping stomach, I had no trouble identifying her womb and cut into it very gently. I didn't want to go too deep and cut into the lamb. Suddenly, as I finished the incision that I realized was much longer than it had to be, the lamb bounced out and thumped onto the straw on the floor.

"Jesus Christ!" Lucien exclaimed in loud surprise.

"Oh, my, he looks so beautiful," Anne Marie said excitedly.

The orange, mucus-covered little blob didn't look particularly beautiful to me and, what was worse, he wasn't moving at all.

"Goddamit, I'm afraid he's a goner," I said. "Here, hold this," I added, handing the knife to Lucien.

I wiped the straw and mucus from around the lamb's muzzle and covered his nose and mouth with my own mouth. The liquid on his muzzle had a rather tangy flavor, not really unpleasant at all.

"Oh, yuck," Anne Marie said, as I breathed in and out into the lamb's nose and mouth.

Suddenly, his back legs kicked once and then again and the lamb jerked his muzzle out of my mouth and blinked his eyes feebly.

"Jesus Christ," I said, "maybe he's gonna make it after all." I patted his head and placed him carefully on a towel I had spread to receive him. He moved his head a bit and weakly tried to look around.

"God, not a very good introduction to the world for you," I said, patting his head.

"You do really good work, Dr. Lew," Anne Marie said excitedly, "but you sure swear a lot."

"No, no, I wasn't swearing," I said, smiling at her. "I was really calling on God and Jesus Christ for a blessing and for help for this poor little fellow." I patted the lamb's head again.

"Here," I continued to Anne Marie, "try to get some of that new milk from the bottle into the little bugger and that should perk him up some. I gotta see if I can get his mother sewed up."

The ewe was bleating feebly, but her movement was much weaker than before. I cauterized the bleeding as best I could and cleaned her womb out a bit. Then, I started with awkward slow stitches to sew up the gaping wound in her womb and stomach.
I was now feeling totally exhausted. My hands were starting to shake and I was having trouble with the stitches.

"Here, let me do it," Anne Marie said. "You men can't sew at all. You feed the lamb and I'll sew her up."

"Sure all right by me," I said with relief. I exchanged places with Anne Marie and squeezed a little milk into the lamb's mouth. His movements were already much stronger than before.

"You two make a great medical team," Lucien said, looking proudly down at his kneeling daughter, who was quickly stitching up the wound I had made. She had less trouble than I had pushing the needle through the ewe's tough skin.

By the time she had finished the stitching and neatly tied off the seam, the lamb was feeling strong enough that I put him back on the towel.

"Surgery over, if that poor ewe doesn't get too bad an infection," I said, bracing myself so I could raise stiffly to my feet. Now that the tension was past, I noticed my feet and my hands weren't feeling as bad as they had before we started working on the ewe.

"God, I sure feel better than I did before we started," I said.

"So now, are you swearing, or are you asking God to help make you feel better?" Anne Marie asked archly.

"Of course I'm asking him to let me feel better," I said.

"You two kids better go up to the house and get some rest," Lucien said. "You both look like you sure as hell need it. I'll stay here and watch this sheep, but you tell that damn Ernie to get his ass out here and relieve me." He released the ewe and untied her legs. She lay limply on her side after the ropes were loosened.

I put my hand over her nose and felt a regular movement of her breath. "She doesn't seem to be dead yet, but I wouldn't count on her chances being too good," I said.

"You kids go in and catch some rest," Lucien said again. "And send Ernie in and I'll fix us all an early breakfast."

Anne Marie kissed her dad and started toward the house. "You go, too, kid," Lucien said to me. "You earned a rest and yuh sure as hell look like you could use it."

"Thanks," I said, as I started to follow Anne Marie. "I've felt more rested, but I really ain't feeling too bad." In fact, the successful birth of the lamb had filled me with an unusual exhilaration. I even jogged a bit on my sore feet to catch up with Anne Marie.

"Well, Nurse Anne, how'd you like the procedure," I asked as I caught up with her.

"It was great fun," she said, taking a bouncy step to illustrate.

"Oh, damn," I said, "I gotta take care of my horse. He needs rest as much as I do."

"I suppose that wasn't swearing either," Anne Marie said playfully. "And if that big buckskin is your horse, he was munching hay in the manger around the barn when I came by."

"I guess I better go take his bridle off and loosen his cinch," I said.

"If you do that, I'll bring him a scoop of oats from the grain bin," Anne Marie said. "There's a grain box over by the manger where he was eating hay. I'll meet you there in a minute."

When I found Yellow Dab, he was munching hay and looking contented. I decided I would take his saddle off so he could get a better rest before we started out again. I threw his saddle and saddle blankets over the manger and hung the bridle over the saddle horn. Just as I finished, Anne Marie threw a scoop of oats into the grain pan. Yellow Dab nickered appreciatively.

"He's really a pretty horse," Anne Marie said. "I admired him a lot at school."

"You sure never said you did," I said. "In fact, I don't remember you ever saying very much of anything at school. You're sure different at home."

"Are you saying I'm too talkative at home?" she asked playfully, smiling her arch smile at me.

"Nah, nah," I said defensively, "I didn't mean that at all."

"Well, don't say it then, Mr. Smart Guy," she replied. "And if it comes to that, you're a lot different at school than you are away from school also. At school you're always so studious and quiet. Mr. Teacher's Pet is what I thought. You and Buddy. Mrs. Swift just likes you big boys best." She skipped ahead of me. "A real book-worm is what I thought of you," she said teasingly over her shoulder.

"Phooey," I said, catching up with her, "you don't have to be a bookworm just because you like to read."

"Well, at least your swearing has improved," she said. "'Phooey' is your mildest curse all night."

"I moderated my language just for your gentle ears," I said, trying to match her gay mood as we entered the house.

Chapter 8

CLOSING THE CIRCLE

The heat from the kitchen stove awakened me. I was curled up on the floor behind the stove with a heavy wool blanket thrown over me. I hadn't even taken my boots off before I went to sleep and my feet were aching unmercifully.

I sat up and wiped the dry corners from my eyes.

"So you're alive after all?" Lucien said. He was sitting at the table drinking coffee with a drowsy smile on his face. "When I came in, I wasn't sure which of you was in worse shape, you or that sheep out there. You were out like a light behind the stove there. Anne Marie tossed the blanket over you. She said you conked out before you could even drink a cup of coffee. You could have used a cot in the bunkhouse, you know. That's where Ernie sleeps. You didn't have to sleep on the floor."

"Nah, it's okay," I said. "I feel a helluva lot better. Just my damn feet hurt pretty bad."

"Well, yuh should pull your boots off fer a spell and give yer dogs some air. I'll fix you a coupla pancakes."

"Nah, that's okay," I said. "I really should be going."

"Shit, kid," he shook his head and stood up. "It ain't even quite daylight yet. You can wait long enough to eat a pancake and some bacon and eggs."

"Yah, all right, thanks," I said, getting stiffly to my feet. I tried to take a step and winced with the pain from my feet.

"Feet really givin' yuh some trouble, eh?" Lucien said sympathetically. "You must have frost-bit 'em a bit. You better git them boots off and take care of 'em."

"I'm afeared if I take 'em off I'll never get 'em on again," I said. "I had 'em off a while last night and my feet were swole up so bad I could barely get 'em back on. I ain't gonna take 'em off again 'til I can leave 'em off awhile." I felt a pang of guilt for my bad grammar. My language seemed to change automatically to fit the company I was with.

"Well, suit yerself, but you better not leave those boots on too damn long," Lucien said, setting a heaping plate of pancakes, bacon, scrambled eggs, and fried potato slices on the table in front of me. "Sit yerself down and have some breakfast anyway." He sat back down at his place and began nursing his coffee again.

I wolfed down a healthy share of the breakfast he had served. "I wonder how that poor ewe is doing," I said, sitting back comfortably and sipping my mug of coffee.

"Yeah, me, too," Anne Marie said, coming in from her room and rubbing her eyes sleepily. "You guys woke me up, and I couldn't stay in bed any longer because of the racket." She looked at us accusingly, but then smiled and kissed her father on the top of his head.

I noticed she was still wearing her flannel nightgown and walking around with bare feet, different from the night before. I guess I'm gaining acceptance as a part of the household, I thought to myself. I couldn't help admiring her shapely feet as she skipped across the room to get herself a cup of coffee.

When she came back to the table, she noticed my stare. "So, you've never seen bare feet before, I suppose, Mr. Hick from the Sticks. I thought Mr., Dr. Lew was supposed to be a cool guy, used to undressed girls."

"Anne Marie," Lucien said mildly, "you stop teasing our guest now and let him finish his breakfast."

"Well, he seems to be finished already," she answered. "He's eaten everything but the plate."

She playfully snipped my hand with her finger to take the sting from her remark. It was the first time she had touched me and I felt my stomach jump.

"I guess I better go have a look at the sheep and relieve Ernie for awhile. He probably could use some breakfast, too," Lucien said, taking his coffee mug to the sink.

"I'll go out with you," I said, sipping the last of my coffee and following his example by placing my mug on the sink. My feet were feeling a little better so I could walk without showing too much pain.

"Wait for me," Anne Marie said, bouncing to her feet, "I want to see how the lamb is doing, too."

"We'll go out and you can dress and catch up with us," Lucien said.

"Unless you want to come out to the barn with bare feet and maybe squish manure between your toes," I said to get back at her.

She stopped and looked at me, taking mock offense. "Well, at least you didn't swear and say the ugly word," she said after a pause. Then, she smiled. "I mean the word 'shit,'" she said, skipping to her bedroom.

"First time I've seen you nearly speechless, since I saw you at school," I said after her as I slipped on my coat and hurried out the door to catch up with her father.

"Anne Marie seems to have taken kind of a likin' to you," Lucien said, as we walked towards the barn.

I was alarmed by the serious tone in his voice. "I hope you

don't mind that I tease her a little," I said. I was afraid he was going to bawl me out.

"Nah, not at all," he said looking at me strangely. "She's got it comin' if ever a girl did."

As we walked through the gate of the corral, he added, "It's just that I've never seen her seem to take to a boy of about her own age before. She's usually totally sullen or shy when boys come around. Or like with Ernie. She doesn't take to most boys at all. Anyway, I'm jist as glad in Ernie's case. I don't think he'd be a very good boy for her to be friends with."

"I better check on Old Yellow Dab, my horse," I said, as I walked across the corral.

"You can give him some oats out of the grain bin over there if you want," he said, still with an odd tone in his voice.

"Nah, better not do that right away," I answered, "Anne Marie gave him a scoop of oats last night. Don't want him to get too much." It was the first time I had spoken her name, and I felt an involuntary jump in my chest as I said it.

Lucien walked to face me and looked up at me with a serious expression. I was a few inches taller than he was, but I felt much younger.

"It's just that I was kinda worried about her," Lucien continued awkwardly, "You know she's always been lots closer to me than to her mother, and I thought that might have made her not so interested in boys her own age." He looked down with an embarrassed expression on his face. "You know what I mean," he added. "Nothin' fer you tuh worry about, I mean. I was just glad she seemed to want to be friends with you. She never said much about you before…when you were both going together to that same Burnham School up there."

"We were in different grades and didn't get much chance to talk to each other," I said. I didn't say we had never talked to each other before, which would have actually been the literal truth. I was about to add that Anne Marie thought I was too much of a book-worm at school, but I decided to keep that to myself as well.

"It's okay, kid, don't lose sleep about it," he clapped his hand against my shoulder and turned to go to the barn.

I wiped Yellow Dab down a bit with a gunny sack that was hanging over the manger.

"I could get you a curry brush and a comb," Anne Marie said to me. I hadn't noticed her leaning over the end of the manger.

"Well, okay, he'd probably love that," I said. She retrieved a large brush and comb from the barn, and we spent a few minutes grooming Yellow Dab, much to his pleasure.

"Jeez, I could use some of that myself," I said, as I finished brushing over his croup.

"There you go, swearing again," Anne Marie said. "Or I suppose you were calling on Jesus to help you with the currying."

"Of course, I was," I said, putting the currying equipment back on the shelf. "I guess we're done unless you want me to curry your braids as well."

"Hah, now he's making fun of my braids," Anne Marie said with mock offense.

"Nah, not me," I said, "I like your braids just the way you got 'em."

"Watch out," she said, poking her finger at me. "Next thing you'll be saying you like me, and we couldn't have that."

"Don't worry about that. I'll never offend your ears by saying anything like that." I was sorry as soon as I said it. She was quiet a minute and I knew I had genuinely hurt her feelings.

"Well, Mr. Smarty Pants," she answered in a subdued tone. "I can say straight and honest, like Jesus tells us. I can say I like you, whether you like me or not, so there."

"I like you, too," I said contritely, "I was just teasing around."

"I knew that right away, before you even said it," she said impudently, skipping ahead of me into the barn.

"We got the lamb nursing fine, but the mother don't look too good," Lucien said, as we reached the stall. Ernie was feeding the lamb some milk from the bottle and it was nursing eagerly. Although she was breathing, the ewe was still lying on her side with her feet splayed away from her body.

"The bleeding seems to have stopped pretty good," I said. "Somebody must have done a good job sewing her up."

When I said it, Anne Marie stuck her tongue out me and then smiled with shy appreciation. Ernie eyed us with a surprised expression on his face.

"We better get her on her feet," I continued. "If she keeps laying on her side like that, she'll never be able to get up, and she'll be dead for sure."

Lucien grabbed the wool on her left side while I reached under her and grabbed the wool on her right side. We lifted her to her feet and planted her on her stiff legs. As soon as we released her, however, her legs began to fold and she started to sink to the floor.

"I think we should hold her on her feet for awhile. Maybe she'll do better if she can stand by herself after awhile." I said hopefully. "Ernie, why don't you bring the lamb over and see if he can stand up and get some milk from her. She had lots of milk in her bag last night."

Ernie stood up sullenly, surprised that I must have sounded like I was giving him orders. As soon as the lamb got near his mother, he stood up eagerly and nosed under her flank looking for a teat. Soon, he was nursing with high energy, his long thin tail whipping back and forth.

"We gotta get rid of that tail, soon," Lucien said, "before he starts to drip lamb shit on it."

"I'd give him a few days before you cut it off," I said. "He's really not too strong yet." I knew Lucien must have been planning to emasculate him also, and I figured that might be too much for him for a few days.

"Yeah, we'll give the little bugger a week or two to recover," Lucien said in a kind tone. "He's been through quite a lot." He changed his stance holding the sheep. "You can take off if you think you hafta," he added. "It's damn near morning as it is, and I can hold her up fine without help. Ernie, you can go grab some breakfast if you want. Anne Marie can help me for a few minutes."

"Glad to, Daddy dear," Anne Marie said. She patted the lamb's back just ahead of his swishing tail. "Oh, he's so cute...so totally cute. He's just darling."

"Yer lettin' that stuck-up little bitch twist you around her finger, too, just like her dad. I wished I could punch the little bitch out myself," Ernie hissed in my ear, as we went out of the barn. "By God, I would, too, except fer her old man. She's sure as hell's got it comin'. That old bastard is too tough fer me, though. Her old man, I mean. I took a swing at him once when he wasn't lookin', and he pounded the holy hell outa me. I didn't think the old half-breed fart had it in him, but he sure beat the shit outa me. Next time, I'll go after him with a fence post, and he won't be so lucky."

"She seems okay to me," I answered him mildly so as not to rile him up any further.

"Where the hell you going?" he asked me as I started to put the bridle on Yellow Dab. "You can't cross the damn river and get home for a few days. You might as well hang around and keep me company. I get lonely as hell out here with just them two half-breeds fer company. You got nothin' better tuh do."

"I gotta get to the school and leave word where I am anyway," I said, "in case my old man shows up looking for me. When I left the school, the teacher thought I was headed home, so they wouldn't know where I was."

"Hell, you worry too much," Ernie answered. "What the hell difference does it make if yer missin' fer a day er two? You ain't alive to please everybody else in the world." I shrugged and he started to turn away. "Unless you got the hots fer that teacher like yer friend Buddy. He tries to pretend like he doesn't like her, but I know damn well better. He'd love up that shrunken leg o' hers and ask fer nothin' better. He wants somethin' she's got and it's shaped a lot like a knot hole."

"You're full of bull shit," I said. "He doesn't even like her at all, and besides he's headed for the army next week."

"Jeez, I didn't know he was leavin' so soon," Ernie said. "But why do you suppose that is," Ernie went on with a laugh. "She won't give him the time o' day, so he joins the army."

"That's total crap," I said. "He joined the army to get away from his old man."

"Maybe, that's part of it," Ernie conceded. "Well, I'm gonna grab some breakfast and some shut-eye before the old fart digs up some other big-assed project fer me tuh do."

"Maybe you should join the army, too, if you want to get away from things," I called after him as he headed towards the house.

"Fat fuckin' chance o' that," he yelled back at me.

"He's just awful," Anne Marie said from the doorway of the

57

barn. "He's always using that f-word. That's just ugly and awful. He's ugly and awful." She paused looking after him. "I just hate that bastard's guts," she added forcefully.

"Whoa, watch that language," I said. "You guys just got winter fever cooped up together here all winter."

"I ain't together with anything with that bastard," she said. "I'd absolutely kill him if I could find a way."

"Jeez," I said, "I think God's got rules against that just as much as against swearing. You need to watch out for your own immortal soul, too, as well as everybody else's."

"Oh, don't be a smarty," she said. "You know what I mean."

"Yah, I guess you didn't mean it seriously," I said, smiling as I tossed my saddle on Yellow Dab's back. "Just like you didn't mean it seriously when you said you liked me."

"Hah!" she said. "So how'd you know I didn't mean that seriously."

"You're just not a serious type person," I said, pulling the cinch tight under Yellow Dab's belly.

"You're right about that," she said. "I've found out it's not good to be too serious in this life."

"You're too young to feel that way," I said. "That's what old fogies are supposed to decide after they've gone through a lot of sh...." I caught myself before I finished the word 'shit.' "...through a lot of crap in their lives," I finished my thought.

"Thank you for being so polite," she said seriously, "and Daddy told me to tell you thanks for all the help you gave us. He still has to hold the ewe up, but he said to come back and stay with us any time you like. You're always welcome."

"I suppose you feel that way, too," I said jokingly.

"Yes, I really do," she said, continuing with her serious tone.

Suddenly, she put her hand delicately on my shoulder and brushed her lips against my cheek. I backed up in shy surprise.

"That's for being a good Dr. Lew and saving that beautiful little lamb," she said. "I almost wish the mother dies, and I'd raise him as my own on the bottle. He'd make a perfect little pet."

I couldn't look at her for a moment. I noticed the pre-dawn sky in the east was developing an off-white halo above the horizon, where the sun would soon be edging over the hills.

"The color of the sacred White Buffalo," I said, pointing towards the horizon.

"Hah, what do you know about the sacred anything," Anne Marie said, glancing over her shoulder. "That's old Indian talk," she added. "But nobody believes that old stuff any more. How do you know about it anyway?"

"You mean young Roman Catholic girls don't believe it," I answered. "But that doesn't mean everybody in the world doesn't believe it. My Grandfather believes in the Old Indian Ways, just as much as my mother believes in being a Catholic, maybe more."

"Oh, your grandfather is the dearest old man I know," Anne Marie said, with real tenderness in her voice. "I feel he's as much my grandfather as he is yours. Every time I see him, I just love him all the more."

"Like someday you're gonna love me," I said, chidingly, with a sudden premonition that must have come from Thunderbird and the bright morning sun, just beginning to show over the river bottom badlands in the southeastern part of the sky.

"Whoa, Mr. Loverboy," in a tone of offense that was clearly feigned. "What in all of God's wonderful Earth and all of God's wonderful Heavens makes you think I would even like you or even think about you..." She paused and then smiled slyly, "...after

59

today, I mean, since I already said I like you today, but that may not last until tomorrow. I may not even remember you tomorrow, Mr. Over-Confident but Insignificant Boy. And what in the wide world makes you even imagine I would ever love you???"

"I know these things," I said, swinging painfully into the saddle. "And besides the White Buffalo is the same color as my old buckskin horse, Yellow Dab here. He tells me these things in telepathic visions of insight and knowledge." I patted Yellow Dab's withers and ran my fingers through his mane straightening out a tangle.

"You better become a better Catholic yourself," she said with firm conviction. "You had just better do that…and then I might consider remembering you…maybe even liking you a little bit more each time I see you, but, then again, maybe I will never again in this world like you better than I do right now, right here today."

"Well, if you might forget me altogether, that would be enough of a blessing that I wouldn't need to be any more Catholic." I smiled at her but I already knew she would know I was just joking and wouldn't take real offense. "Besides, in our household my mother takes care of all Catholic issues and observances, so the rest of us don't have to bother. My grandmother takes care of all Adventist issues since she's an Adventist, and Adventists are very suspicious of all Catholics. And my Grandfather takes care of all sacred issues concerning the Sacred White Buffalo and the very Powerful Thunderbirds. And I help him out a lot and learn from him. And my father believes in the absolute equality of all religions, whatever you believe in. I think he pretty much hates all religions equally, but I'm not sure about that."

"Hates religion?" Anne Marie said with genuine shock in her voice. "I can't believe that, at all. It ain't possible to hate all religions." She paused a minute and with a twinkle added, "There, now see what you made me do with your silly religion talk."

"What?" I asked, genuinely mystified. "What bad thing did I make you do?"

"You made me commit a bad 'ain't' error, when I certainly learned better from Mrs. Swift. You shocked me so bad I said 'ain't', when I should have said very distinctly and firmly, 'It is not possible to hate all religions." We smiled at each other, both somewhat equally surprised, I think, at our new-found affection for each other's company.

"So long," she said, putting her hand up to wave goodbye. I mistook her gesture and reached out to shake her hand. When I realized my mistake, I brushed my lips across the back of her hand to cover my embarrassment.

"My, the gallant gentleman," she said, pulling her hand away with a smile. "A real knight in shining armor. I didn't know gentlemen were supposed to kiss lady's hands anymore. It's kind of neat, anyway. Now, I can be the lady-in-waiting, while my gallant warrior goes off on a quest. Maybe, you can bring me home a baby dragon after you slay the fearsome, fire-breathing mother, like you guys were reading in 'Beowulf' in class."

"So you were listening to us big students read about the gallant warriors," I said.

"Well, I was listening when you read," she answered. "I couldn't understand what those other guys were saying at all when they were trying to read aloud. Wow, especially Lyle. I can never understand a word he says."

"He can talk okay," I said. "But he can't read at all. That's why the teacher just lets him make up sounds when he's supposed to be reading aloud. I guess she doesn't want him to get too embarrassed.

But notice she cuts him off right away and doesn't let him waste too much time, acting like he's reading."

"Ernie isn't really much better with his reading," Anne Marie added. "I can read ten times, a hundred times better than him. Buddy reads pretty good. But I really listen to you. Every time you read, I stop whatever I'm doing and listen to you. You're a great reader and give great expression to the words. We go to Episcopal Church sometimes, and you sound a lot like the minister there, preaching his sermon. My mom's an Episcopal, you know."

"My great grandfather was an Episcopal," I said. "He went to school in England."

"Ah," she said, "see, you should be an Episcopal. Then, you could preach great sermons and save many souls, and even I would listen to you with awe and admiration, and I would say to the whole world, 'I knew that great preacher in school when we were students together,' and he was just a stupid boy."

"Stupid now, is it?" I said with mock offense. "Mrs. Swift would not like to hear you say that about her smartest student. Boy student, that is. There might be one girl in the class that has half a brain anyway, but I don't know who it would be."

"Enough, Mr. Smarty Pants," she said with a sweet smile of surrender in the rivalry of words, "Anyway, I like Mrs. Swift a lot," she said. "She's lots better than that old teacher we had before. The one who got sick."

I didn't tell her that the old lady teacher we had before was my Aunt Esther Neiber. We'd never said anything about that at school.

"I guess she's okay. Mrs. Swift, I mean, not Mrs. Neiber," I answered.

"You just don't want to admit how great she is because she's a woman, and you bright boys can't stand girls who are even smarter than they are. It's too much for their phony pride to bear."

"Mrs. Swift should be smarter than me 'cause she's older," I said. "And besides she's been to college and I haven't even been to high school."

"But you'll go, of course," Anne Marie said firmly. "And she isn't that much older than you, anyway. She's only a year older than Buddy, I heard him say one day to Ernie, and I don't know how much older Buddy is than you."

"A few years," I said, vaguely at a loss for more to say.

Her complete confidence in me to go to high school, to do what was still a vague hope in my mind made my heart pound with a burst of sudden affection for her—and a sudden loss of words.

There was an awkward pause. I realized I didn't want to leave nearly as much as I had a few hours before.

"Well, I better hit the trail," I said finally. "I'll probably try to drop back to see you guys after I let them know at school where I am."

"I'm really glad you stopped in," she said as I turned Yellow Dab towards the sunrise. "Even if you're only coming back to see the 'guys,' rather than me." I heard her tinkling laughter follow me, as I kicked Yellow Dab into a trot.

Chapter 9

CONTINUING THE CIRCLE

Yellow Dab was full of piss and vinegar after all the oats he'd gotten in the last day — "You act like you got a coffee high on oats," I said to him, as we trotted up the graded county road that led out of the river bottom to the bench land above. The county road wound back and forth finding the easiest route south through the clay buttes.

"Damn, it's gonna be a nice spring day after all," I said to no one in particular. We hit the bench land about that same moment. The bright disc of the sun was just cracking above the southeast horizon over the gentle blue volcanic peaks of the Bearpaw Mountains. Rays of sun were flashing across the small patches of snow that still dotted the prairie.

"God, it's beautiful," I said, throwing my arms out with one rein in each hand. Yellow Dab laid his ears back at my exuberance, but he kept up the same steady trot without wavering. We hadn't gone this way before, but he liked the easy flat road.

I was just about to turn left at the intersection of the county road that led back to Burnham School when I saw a light on at the roadhouse that was a half mile or more ahead, where the county road we were on intersected Highway 2.

"Jesus, what's goin' on up there at this time of day?" I asked Yellow Dab. I stopped him for a minute at the intersection of the county road. "Goddam, we should go up and have a look," I told him. "We're both pretty damn tired," I told him, trying to rationalize my decision to myself. "But what the hell! It's still early as hell. I probably couldn't get into the school if we got there now anyway." I knew that likely wasn't true because the outside school door had never been locked as long as I could remember. I didn't even know if it had a lock.

"It must have a padlock or something on the outside so they can lock it through the summer," I told Yellow Dab. "But Mrs. Swift couldn't lock that up from the inside anyway," I added, looking at both sides of the argument.

"But maybe she sets a lock or something or braces a chair against the door when she's there alone at night," I argued to Yellow Dab.

"Oh, hell," I said, tired of the indecision, "it's only half a mile and maybe she'll be up by the time we get there if it ain't so early." I guided Yellow Dab down the road we were on towards the roadhouse. "Christ," I thought to myself, "you just as well admit up front that you're leery about getting there before she gets up."

"It ain't like when I sleep in the cloakroom," I told Yellow Dab. "Then, she lets us know when she's got some breakfast ready so we don't disturb her before she's out of bed."

By the time I finished the discussion with Yellow Dab, he had carried us up to the roadhouse, where the sign was flashing "Fresno Inn and Bar." The light reflected across a mound of dirty snow in the parking lot that had been heaped up around the base of the signpost.

I rode Yellow Dab around to the back of the tavern, where there was a shabby little stable for the few riders who might still come by to wet their whistles, as the saying goes. I loosened Yellow Dab's cinch and took off his bridle and patted his ass as he trotted into an open stall. I latched the stall gate behind him. "I'll toss you a little hay," I told him. I felt bad after I looked at the musty shit I had to throw him for hay. "I suppose you'll turn up your nose at this," I admitted to him. "But it's the best we can do."

I left the stable and walked around the building to the side door of the roadhouse. As I was about to try the door, I heard a noise out back again. I hurried back around the corner towards the stable and saw the owner, whose name I couldn't remember, throwing a dishpan full of dirty dishwater into the back parking lot.

"Goddam, you startled the hell outa me," he said, almost dropping the dishpan. "I thought you were one of them goddam partiers still hangin' around. Jesus Christ, I thought they'd never clear out last night. Come on in, then, and have a cup o' coffee. I got a whole pot brewed…and I hate tuh drink alone."

"Jesus Christ," he said again, chortling at his own joke. He held the door open and showed me a seat at the small round table, where he placed a cup of coffee. "Christ, we had one helluva party last night," he went on, washing another load of dishes as he talked.

"A goddam wedding party," he went on. "They're always a bitch but they're a lot of fun. Jesus Christ, some young kid marryin' a divorcee, if yuh wanna know. Christ, she's married and divorced a time or two and got two kids. Kids damn near as old as the groom, for Chissake. I don' know what to make of kids nowadays. By god, no kids in my day was gonna marry old battleaxes that was twice their ages…goddam, with two damn young sprouts at that. Hell's bells!"

He saw my interest perk up as he went on with his story. "Jesus Christ, maybe you know this kid. You go to Burnham School right over across the tracks there, don'tcha. By God, I know this kid's parents real well. They's in here all the time, that's why he got aholt o' me for the wedding party.

"Course I've knowed the bride fer years. Damn lush is in here ever' night er two, swilling it up and flirtin' with the cowboys and raisin' hell. Christ, I know she works, but I think she probably makes more money after the bar closes, spreading her legs fer some cowboy er other. Fer money, too, I's heard. I heard she takes money fer fuckin' around. That's bad shit any way yuh look at it, Good Christ. Damn whore. Ain't gonna be too good fer that kid she's married up with. She's been married who knows how many times before and fuckin' around alls the time—fer money at that. Good God!"

He paused and shook his head disapprovingly, so I could finally get in a word. "What's the kid's name, the bridegroom?" I asked. "It ain't Buddy Morse, is it?"

"Yeah, yeah, that's who it is. His folks farm out south here and he jus' graduated from eighth grade at Burnham School, I think he said." He picked up another dishpan full of dirty dishwater and started towards the backdoor with it. "Christ, ask him yerself. He and the 'blushing bride' o' his are sleepin' it off at one of the back booths in the main barroom there," he nodded towards the door to the bar. "Just go on in and kick their asses awake. They gotta get outa here soon anyway. Christ, it's morning. I could be in a shit pot full o' trouble if the cops was to stop in. Well, they never come by this time o' day much, unless it's a goddam emergency, or what not. Christ almighty, I don't even think that kid's of age. He's jus' graduated from eighth grade and he says he already joined the Marines, 'n he's marryin' that whorin' bitch. Jeez Christ!" I heard him repeat, "What's the goddam modern world comin' to anyway. Goddam sheriff sometimes stops in fer coffee early, too, Jesus

Christ. He's raising holy hell if that damn kid, the groom's still here, Christ s'mighty." He snorted as he slammed the door behind himself.

I grabbed up my coffee and hurried through the door into the barroom. I couldn't make out anything until my eyes had adjusted to the gloom. I looked around the big room and finally spotted Buddy smoking a cigarette at one of the back booths. I started towards him. I paused a minute because I didn't want to intrude, but he waved me over when he recognized me.

"Jesus Christ, my old pal," his voice was a little slurred. "Jeez, yer my oldest friend, you know that. My parents heard you'd been born almost the same day it happened, and they dragged me in to the hospital fur uh visit. Chris', I dunno how you could've got so ugly now when you wuz so cute then. You wasn't much of a crybaby, even when you wuz on'y 'bout a foot long. Christ, that's one of the things I al'ays liked 'bout you, you never cried aroun' about yer misfortunes, and shit like that. Christ, and yer fuckin' old man is just as fuckin' bad as mine. Goddam, ain't they both mean old sons-o'-bitches. The Marine Corps will be a fuckin' picnic after livin' with my old man all these years, Jesus Christ."

"You've only told me that story about four hundred times," I said, "and besides you know goddam well I get cuter every goddam day, so you might as well give up tryna convince me otherwise. You're just afeard I'll outshine you too goddam much. That's why you have to keep tellin' me that story about how ugly I turned out. You ain't exactly a cute bastard yourself."

"Maybe, that's the truth, ol' buddy o' Buddy's. Maybe, you hit the nail on the head right there. I'll be damned. From the mouth o' babes comes wisdom, er some shit like that. You know, that's why I di'nt invite you to the wedding or even tell you about it er nothin'. Yer so damn young you couldn'a come to the party and drunk nothin' anyway. Chris', if you wasn' so damn tall, you'd look like you was about in second grade or so. Christ on a Cross, I tell you no lie." He paused and took a long puff on his butt, then got out a pack of Lucky Strikes and lit himself another cigarette. He started to offer me one, but then remembered I didn't smoke and stuck the pack back into his pocket.

"Besides," he added, "I didn' even know fer sure I was gonna go through with it 'til after I got home yesterday. My goddam ol' man kicked me outa the house fer a graduation present, so I went over to Joyce's and one thing led to another and, pretty soon, we's decided we're gonna get hitched. We'd been talkin' 'bout it fer quite awhile anyways, yuh know. So we called all our friends we could get ahold of and organized a party. We're gettin' hitched about Monday—er probably Tuesday—so youse can come if yuh want. We gotta get it done before I head for basic training next week."

"Jesus Christ, you're marrying Joyce Carruthers, is it?" I asked him with my lower lip resting on my chin.

"Hell, yes, my friend, good ol' Joyce, you must've met her. Christ, there isn't a man in Hill County who hasn't had the hots for her at one time or another. Don't think I don't know that well enough. But she's marryin' me, by God. Son-of-a-bitch, what d'ya think o' that fer the knave's good fortune. She's the prettiest goddam thing in Montana, fer Chissakes! Only trouble is, I'll be beatin' off every night in boot camp over her goddam picture. Son-of-a-bitch, you gotta come over here and say hello and congratulate her." He started to lead me towards the booth where Joyce Carruthers was still snoring her life away.

"Well, I dunno," I answered, holding back. Joyce Carruthers was about the most beautiful woman I had ever seen in my life. She was statuesquely tall with bright laughing blue eyes and long majestically blonde hair. When I was working through the summers with my dad in Bull Hook at the Bull Hook Livestock Commission, she was the bookkeeper in the Commission office. When my dad would take me with him to the bars after work, we would usually meet up with her. She liked my dad a lot, I could tell. I guess it was because he was such a bundle of nervous energy and could tell great stories that would make her laugh all evening long.

Sometimes on those nights, I would go to the movies and then to an all-night cafe, where I'd sip tea and read Ernest Hemingway or somebody until my dad got around to picking me up. Usually, I'd fall asleep in the booth before he came by. Sometimes, it would be early morning before he'd make it to the cafe to get me up for the long drive home. He was always in good humor while spending an evening with Joyce hitting the bars and whatever else. But he was always drunk by the time he picked me up, so we'd have a wild ride home through the Milk River Breaks up the single track country road that led us through the badlands to the ranch that my grandfather had originally homesteaded on and that my father was now running.

My father was probably a pretty fun guy as far as Joyce was concerned, but he was one mean son-of-bitch after he'd spent an evening drinking with her. It probably wasn't her fault anyway.

He was a mean son-of-a-bitch most of the time, whenever he was away from his friends. His family he could treat like shit, I thought bitterly, but friends like Joyce he treated like royalty.

I figured it was probably because he really wanted to spend his time with Joyce and her drinking buddies, rather than me and my mother and the rest of the family. I liked it when he spent time with Joyce because it always cheered him up, but it really pissed me off when he was so fucking grouchy afterwards.

Joyce had always treated me really well anyway. Whenever I'd run into her, she'd put her arm around my shoulder and order me a ginger ale from the bartender. Little Lew, she always called me as she patted my back. "Little Lew, you'll be a heart-breaker someday. You're as handsome as a movie star. I bet you look just like Gary Cooper did when he was a kid." Then, she'd ruffle my hair and kiss my cheek. It always left a faint stain of red lipstick on my cheek. Unlike Anne Marie's sweet kiss, I thought.

Joyce Carruthers! Did I know her? Jesus Christ, I hadn't seen her for a few years now, but I had been madly in love with her since the first time I'd met her in the bar in summer when I was "just a stripling," as Shakespeare would have said it. She was the ideal of all worldly beauty as far as I was concerned, Desdemona for damn sure. But I wouldn't take her for virginal Juliet, I thought to myself with a smile. Jesus help me, the minute I realized who Buddy was marrying, I was instantly jealous as hell and half hated his guts, even if I was his oldest friend…and he certainly was my oldest friend at that, just like he said.

"C'mon, Joyce, wake up," Buddy said, going to where Joyce was laid out prone in one of the booths. She was lying down asleep in a booth with her long trim legs in elegant high pink heels hanging into the aisle. Her navy blue, square-dance skirt was tossed up so I could see the tops of her light beige nylon stockings. Her head was hanging to the side, and she was snoring softly through her wide-open mouth, a drop of spit or phlegm lodged against the corner of her lip. Her soft white sweater was pulled loose from her skirt waist, and I could see a wide strip of her curvy pale stomach moving up and down with her breathing.

"Joy, come on, meet my best friend," Buddy said. "He's gonna be your protector while I'm away in the army. He'll look out for you and check on you while I'm away saving the world from the Communist hordes." He shook her awake, and she sat up looking around the room with bleary eyes. When she spotted me, she squinted at me but didn't seem to recognize me.

"Damn," she said, "where's my damn glasses? I can't make out anything over two feet away without my glasses." She fumbled for her glasses, which had elegant tortoise-shell frames.

When she had them on, she stared at me again. "God almighty," she said, rubbing her eyes in disbelief, "Could that be Little Lew!? My God, you're all grown up. And by God, you're handsome as ever. I knew you'd grow up to be a handsome devil heartbreaker. You're the very devil's own son, and your dad is sure one helluva heartbreaker. Like father, like son." She said this with a slight tone of bitterness. Her voice sounded almost like a man's, but a little higher pitched. Even after just waking up from a hard night, her pronunciation was precise and articulate.

"She's around men all the time, ranchers and hicks and cowboys that hung out at the livestock commission company where she worked," I thought, "so it's not surprising she'd start to talk like a man."

"Christ, it's damn good to see you, Little Lew, even when I'm something of a mess. We had a helluva party last night. Really shook the rafters of this dump, I tell you. Good thing we were way out of town or we'd never have gotten away with it. We'd all have spent the night in jail." She stood up and patted her skirt straight and tucked her sweater in at the waist. She took a comb from her purse on the table and whipped it quickly through her hair, then a small hand mirror to check her makeup and add a swipe of lipstick. Suddenly, she was transformed before our eyes into what could have passed for an elegant professional woman on her way to her own uptown office.

"Damn, Little Lew, it's great to see you." She opened her arms, "Damn, you get over here and give me a big hug and a kiss. You should be celebrating my wedding like everybody else."

She stepped towards me and engulfed me in a tight embrace. I was tense as ever to be "pawed over by a damn woman," as my dad would have put it. But she was having none of my trepidation.

"Relax and enjoy yourself, Lew," she whispered in my ear. "Hell, you're damn near grown up. It's time you learned to relax and enjoy the feel of a woman." She was nearly as tall as me, in her high-heeled pink shoes. She held onto me until I finally raised my arms and put them around her waist. She gave me an extravagant kiss on the mouth, which jarred my hat loose.

"All right, that's better," she said approvingly, as she stepped back. "Young guys need to learn to enjoy themselves with women, just like women need to learn to pleasure themselves with guys."

"Hell, Sweetheart...," she continued, turning her attention to Buddy and giving him the same hug and kiss she had given me. "But not with quite as much enthusiasm," I thought to myself jealously. "You know damn well I got plenty of interest about pleasuring myself with a man, don't you, honey," she finished her statement and stepped back and patted Buddy's cheek.

Both Buddy and I stood speechless, staring at her in open admiration. I could feel an erection bursting against the placket of my overalls, so I was glad I had my coat zipped up, then no one would notice.

"Well, I gotta hit the john and the kitchen for some Java, if you handsome young dudes will excuse me," she said, walking towards the kitchen with the long, easy stride that made her look like she was in charge of the entire world—and especially of all the men in it.

Both Buddy and I stood in speechless admiration while we watched her leave. "Damn, she's beautiful," Buddy said with admiration in his voice. "Look at that ass on her. Christ, it looks like it's gonna break away from the rest of her the way it waves back and forth atcha."

"Well, congratulations, I guess I should say," I said, not quite able to keep down a slight tone of bitterness.

"Shit, I guess so," Buddy said with a tone of discouragement in his voice. He grabbed up a beer and walked across to a far booth.

"What the hell's wrong?" I asked, following him. "Christ, you marry the damnedest most beautiful lady in the country, and you sound like you're about ready to shit a brick." I clapped him on the back. "Smile, for Christ's sake," I added to cheer him up.

He sat in a far booth, sipping the beer. I sat across from him with my cup of coffee.

"Great Falls Select," I read the label of his beer bottle, "the Champagne of Bottled Beer."

"Shit," Buddy said, "it tastes more like shit than champagne."

I sipped my coffee. "Christ," Buddy said, "why don't you get a beer—or some of that sour shit punch outa that bowl over there—and join the fuckin' party."

"Naw, it's a little early fer that," I answered. I didn't like beer much anyway, and the punch bowl was a murky pink color. "Besides, who wants to drink with a gloomy bastard like you?"

"Shit, Lew, yer right. Yer my best friend in the world—maybe my only goddam friend, for Chrissake—and I'm gonna level with you. My life is turning to absolute shit before my very eyes." His earlier drunken slur had cleared up with amazing speed, I thought.

"Christ, everything I do seems to make things worse." Buddy went on. "I try to get things straightened out and they jus' git worse. Everything gets more and more fucked up, the more I try to straighten it out."

"I don't see it," I said. "Christ, you graduated yesterday—and got a real diploma, unlike Lyle. Then, you're in the Marines, which I know you always wanted to do. Now, to top it off, you're marrying the most beautiful lady in the country. You should be smiling your ass off. Jesus Christ, if you're so gloomy with what's happened to you for the last few days, by comparison the rest of the goddam world would be committing suicide, if they were reacting to their fortune or misfortune like you are, for Chrissake."

"Well, shit, Lew," Buddy answered me, with tears coming to his eyes. He wiped them away angrily. "I just haven't leveled with you about the whole story is all. Christ, I knew my old man was gonna give me the boot. That's been brewin' fer a long time, and I don't give a shit about it. Good riddance to the old bastard, I say, if he don't want me around. Hell, I got the Marine Corps now anyway; that's probably better than my home, as it is. My former home, that is. The old bastard couldn't even wait a couple of days 'til I left for basic training and I woulda been outa the house without him havin' t' kick me out. Shit!"

"So you're gittin' what you want anyway. You're away from your old man, and now you're gonna marry the movie star of this country and, what the hell, you look like you just lost your last goddam friend." I poked his arm to cheer him up. "Hell, I'm still your goddam friend despite however many good reasons I have to kick your ass." I poked his arm until he had to look at me. But he still wouldn't move or even retaliate against my picking on him.

Joyce came back into the bar, swaying towards us balancing a full cup of coffee. My heart bounced into my throat just at the sight of her.

"Give us a break," Buddy said to Joyce with a loud grouch in his voice. "We got important man-talk goin' on here. Grab another chair for awhile." Buddy dismissed her with a wave of his hand.

Joyce looked totally shocked. She stopped uncertainly, slopping a little coffee from her cup, then turned abruptly and went back to the kitchen without saying anything.

"Jesus Christ," I said angrily, "that was sure as hell uncalled for."

"Shit," Buddy said shrugging, "if she's gonna be my ol' lady, she better get used to takin' orders. She's gotta learn who's boss." He took a long pull on his bottle of Budweiser.

"Christ," he continued with a more cheerful note in his voice, "did you see her bounce outa here. I already got that Marine command presence. Shit, she wouldn't dare talk back."

"Yeah," I answered, "that'll last about thirty-eight seconds with her. She'll either kick your ass or be out the door." He just smirked morosely and took another drink of his beer. "Shit," I said, determined to get through to him. "You know who you fuckin' sound like. You sound just like your old man—or better yet even—my old man. Is that the kind of shithead you want to be all your life?"

He actually started to cry and bowed his head down so I wouldn't see. I'd never seen him really cry before. I got out of my booth and stood awkwardly for a minute. Finally, I punched his arm gently. "Hey, man," I said. "You ain't never gonna be like your old man—or my old man. Shit, I know you better'n that. Hell, I spoke outa turn."

I sat back down and watched him awkwardly clear his tears.

"Shit, I know she's marryin' me 'cause of the Marine allowance for dependents. Jesus, I know that. Christ, so she's got two kids, and she doesn't make any damn money down at that Bearpaw Livestock Commission job she's got. Hell, you parttime kids that work down there make damn near as much as she does. So hell, I don't mind that, Christ." He sat back and took a swig of beer and shook out a Lucky Strike.

"And Christ, she's a beauty and a great piece of ass," Buddy went on with a little more enthusiasm. "Hell, and I fuckin' kid you not, she's the best goddam piece of ass in the world."

Buddy smiled at his own remark, and maybe about the night before and other great nights to come, but his mood shifted immediately back to total melancholy. "How would I know she's a great piece of ass?" he said. "She's the only piece of ass I've ever had. How would I know how good she is. I've got nothin' to compare her to."

"I don't think you need comparisons," I said. "Just looking at her must be better than shackin' with most girls. I speak from far wider experience than yours, of course."

"Shit, you're totally full of shit and you know it," Buddy said, smiling a bit despite himself. "You're a fuckin' virgin if there ever was one. I doubt you ever even kissed a real woman."

"Shit," I answered, with a pang at the truth of his remark, "you damn well know better than that. You saw Joyce kiss me just like she kissed you, not ten minutes ago."

"Christ, I mean a little more than a sloppy kiss, for Chrissake," he said shaking his head with a genuine laugh. "Listen, hotshot ladykiller, you have my fuckin' permission to make out with Joyce anytime you want, whether we're married or not…as long as I'm not in bed with her. I ain't quite ready to go two in a bed with her yet."

"Why not," I said jokingly. "You keep sayin' I'm yer best

friend. Then, when the chips are down and you could really show your friendship, you renege and won't go through with it. Some fair weather friend you are."

"Fuck you," he said, with a genuine smile, "and I did mean it when I said I wanted you to look out for her when I'm gone. Hell, I owe her that at least. Check on her every few days if you get a chance. She's got those two kids to take care of and she blows her fuckin' money like it was water. She's always fuckin' busted. Since I met her, I don't think she's ever had two bucks to rub together at the same time. She blows her money as soon as she gets it. You check on her, would ya' and make sure she and the kids are doin' okay."

"Yeah, sure," I said. "I know pretty close where her apartment is there in Bull Hook. I'll check on her every chance I get."

"Thanks, old pal," Buddy said in a light voice, "and, fer Chrissake, sleep with her, too, if she'll let you, and she probably will," he stopped gloomily. "If you feel like you want to, that is," he said more lightly to regain a better mood. "I wouldn't want to push you into anythin' you really din't want to do. Shit, better if she fucks you than some of the other shitheads she goes around with."

"Is that what's botherin' you, for Chrissake," I pressed him. "You say the fact that she might — 'might,' I emphasize—sleep around, then you say you don't care if she does. But you still look like the end of the world was upon us. What the hell's goin' on anyway?" He looked away and avoided my look.

We sat quietly for a moment. "Christ," he said with a serious tone in his voice, "I might as well tell you the fuckin' truth. I gonna be leavin' the country in a coupla days anyway, so what the hell difference does it make who knows. The whole world could know, as far as I'm concerned and I wouldn't give a damn about it."

I leaned my head back against the back of the booth and looked at the ceiling. "You're one balky bastard," I said disgustedly. "If you got something to say, spill it and quit acting like you're drinking curdled milk."

He leaned forward folding his arms on the table and looked at me seriously. "I'm in love," he said with great sincerity. There was a pause.

"I know you're in love. You're marryin' Joyce in a couple of days, so what's the problem?"

"No, you don't understand," he went on just as sincerely as before. "I'm not in love with Joyce at all. I feel sorry for her and I like her kids a lot and all that. I wanna make sure she's all right, so I mean it when I say you need to watch out for her."

"Jesus Christ," I said disgustedly, "you told me that three times at least. I'll take care of her as best I can and as much as she and her kids might need, if it comes to that, so what's the problem? I'm not even surprised you're not in love with Joyce. You just got hot pants for her. Shit, you don't even act like you're in love with her." I paused and added with what I realized was probably a considerable understatement, "Christ, I'm sure I'm probably more in love with her than you are." I felt a pang even as I said it. "Christ," I said to myself, "that's an understatement if I ever heard one. I'm completely and hopelessly in love with Joyce."

Another long pause! "So what are we here? In a big sob story like 'The Perils of Pauline' or some other damn tear-jerker? Are you fuckin' gonna tell me what's goin' on or do I have to beat it out of you?" I got up and started to leave.

"Christ," he called after me, "Come on back. I need to tell somebody before I leave for the army and get my ass shot off er somethin'."

After I sat back down, he leaned toward me seriously again.

"Christ, you won't fuckin' believe this and you gotta promise not to tell a soul," he paused long enough for me to nod. "I'm in love with Mrs. Swift. Stephanie, that is. That's her first name." He looked down at the table and rubbed his hands in what appeared to be a kind of despair. "Madly and completely in love. I want to be with her every minute of the day. I never want to see anyone else. Just her. I want to take her with me everywhere. I can't get along without her." He paused out of breath. "It's hopeless," he finally added.

"Christ, we are in the midst of 'The Perils of Pauline'," I said, "Where are the goddam soaring violins when you need 'em?"

Chapter 10

GRADUATION PRESENT

"How could you be in love with her—Stephanie, I mean?" I asked Buddy. "All I've heard you do for the last month is bitch about her. That don't look much like love to me."

"Hell, no," Buddy answered, "that is love. Would I be bitchin' so much about her if I didn't love her?"

"Don't ask me," I said. "You're the one that's got two women on the string. You must be the expert on love, more than me."

"Shit, listen to me and learn somethin'. Have I always bitched about her? No! When she first took over for ol' Mrs. What's-her-name, when that ol' bitch got sick, did I bitch about her? Hell, no! I wanted to make out with her ten minutes after I first saw her. And that hasn't changed a damn bit since I first saw her either."

"Gimme a break," I answered him. "Just cause you wanted to make out with her doesn't mean you have to be in love with her."

"Listen to Mr. Expert on the affairs of the heart," Buddy said. "You goddam virgin, you don't know anything."

"So instruct me, Mr. Know-it-all," I said, "...if you think my virgin ears can stand it."

"Hell, the first step to being in love is that you want to fuck some bitch," Buddy answered earnestly, "then you want to spend all your time with 'em, then you want to do things for 'em. Like that."

"Sure," I said. "I just heard you say you wanted to take care of Joyce, too—or you want me to while you're gone. You tell me how beautiful Joyce is; then you tell me you don't love her. You love this schoolmarm, Stephanie, instead. What kinda sense is that?"

"Shit, grow up, virgin," Buddy said. "Love don't have to make sense. If it did, then it wouldn't be real love. And don't you say anything bad about Stephanie or, by God, I'll clock you one."

"You'll 'try to clock me one' is what you mean," I said, rising to my feet. "And while you're 'trying', I'll be knockin, you ass over teakettle and throwin' your sorry Marine ass in the snow bank by the tavern sign out front."

"Oh, sit down, you sorry asshole," he answered. "Don't think I didn't see your long face when you found out I was marryin' Joyce. Shit, marry her yerself if you want to. I don't give that much of a shit about it one way or another. I'll find plenty of younger ass in the Marine Corps. I don' need Joyce to throw her cunt around at me. She throws it at every other son-of-a-bitch, anyway. What the hell do I care?"

"Shit," I said mournfully, leaning my head into my arms on the table. "She won't marry me cuz I couldn't get any goddam Marine allowance for her and her kids like you can. That's probably the only damn reason she's marryin' you anyway."

"Fuck," he said, "what do I care why she's marryin' me—if she's even gonna go through with it? It doesn't mean shit to me." Suddenly, he leaned forward with an evil grin. "Why don't you join the Marines with me and then you can get the goddam allowance—and then maybe she'd give you the time o' day, too."

"Fuck you," I said. "I'm goin' to high school and we'll see who she gives the time o' day to when I graduate."

"If you graduate, bonehead!" He pushed my head up out of my arms. "Besides I'm gonna take classes in the Marine Corps and finish high school ahead of you anyway."

"Listen," he went on. "Remember when Mrs. Swift—Stephanie, that is—first came to teach at Burnham. Hell, I couldn't keep my eyes off the cute little bitch. She'd start with her high falutin' shit, and I'd just sit there with my mouth open, hopin' she'd just look at me. Jesus Christ! I had it bad. Remember those bad weather nights when we had to stay in the cloakroom. Shit, I loved those nights. You'd be out fuckin' around, curryin' yer horse, and I'd be in the classroom tryna fuck the teacher. Shit, that's not true. I was in the classroom all right, but I was just tryna git her t' talk t' me, t' notice me. And shit, she never would. She never gave me the slightest damn tumble. Oh, she'd talk to me, all right—about gitting an education 'n shit like that. She even told me about her marriage and about her accident. About how her husband had been this 'sweet sensitive musician guy,' who made her feel like a princess." Mockingly, he tried to imitate the sound of her voice. "Not what I wanted to talk about, fer damn sure."

"'Buddy, you need to think about your future. You need to consider going on to high school,' she'd say. To hell with her and her damn high school is what I decided." He looked morosely at the floor.

"So what about her husband anyway?" I said with sudden interest. "Where the hell is he? He never seems to come to see her or nothin'."

"Shit, he left her as soon as she had her accident. She had a long period of recovery and therapy and shit, so's she could walk on her leg. So he dumped her."

"Well, she really is pretty cute at that," I said, remembering the hug she'd given me before I fled the schoolroom. "Except for that shrunken leg." I couldn't help but rub it in to Buddy a little bit. "After all, he's stealing Joyce, the love of my life," I thought to myself. "He deserves a little shit."

"'Cute' ain't the word for it. I seen that bitch naked, whether you believe it or not. And she's got bazooms as big as Mae West. And they stand right up. No saggy flesh on her. Joyce is gittin' a little saggy, yuh know. Too old and too much drinkin' and shit. But Stephanie, by God, she's trim as a goddam Olympic runner. Big boobs and, by God, she's cute from head to foot, just her calf is shrunken up a little bit…which I think gives her a big complex about her looks. She thinks she doesn't measure up." He leaned back in the booth and looked his admiration of Stephanie at the ceiling.

"Okay, okay," I said, "I believe you're head over heals in fuckin' love. Now, what the fuck are you gonna do about it? Marry Joyce, who you don't love, instead of Stephanie, who you do love."

"'Whom,' you dumb fuck. 'Whom' you don't love. 'Whom' you do love," Buddy said with a smirk. "Marines don't have to know that shit, but how you gonna get to high school if you haven't got 'who-whom' straight?"

"Yeah, yeah, I know 'who-whom'," I said, "and you'll do any damn thing to change the subject. What about you goin' and askin' Stephanie to marry you or wait for you or something, instead of marryin' Joyce?"

"Hell, no, couldn't do it," he said. "Listen, let me tell you what happened a coupla months ago when I saw Mrs. Swift—Stephanie, that is—naked for the first and one and only time. Before that happened, I decided I was gonna tell Stephanie I loved her, wanted her, if she would only wait for me while I was in the Marine Corps or if she could maybe join me somewhere after I got settled into a unit. Jeez, I'd even applied for duty in Hawaii cuz I figgered that'd make her happy.

"So I thought I'd git to school early one morning and tell her how I felt, and would she join me in Hawaii when I got assigned there. Hell, I figgered she couldn't turn down Hawaii, Jesus Christ."

"So I got to school and put Paint into the barn and figgered I'd sneak in quiet and talk to Mrs. Swi' — Stephanie—before anyone got to school...."

"'Anyone else'," I said to irritate him. "'Anyone else arrived at school' would be better grammar."

He looked at me with a blank expression for a minute, then ignored making a retaliation and went on with his story.

"Anyway, I opened the school door and there she was naked as hell at the washstand, scrubbin' herself down with a washcloth. She noticed the sound of my coming through the door and turned towards me with her two breasts stuck out in my direction like two big melons with rosy tits that seemed to point right at me. She didn't even try to cover the triangle of cunt hair under the round little soft bulge of her tummy.

"I was struck speechless at the sight of her. I couldn't even catch my breath. I just stood and stared."

"'Would you please wait outside and wait till I finish dressing and ring the school bell?' she said. 'And please knock before you come in again.' She didn't even try to cover herself, for God's sake. She just continued dryin' herself until I could catch my breath and turn around and shut the door behind myself. I couldn't even bring myself to go near her when she's alone since that day, but I couldn't change my feelin's for her. I just fell more and more in love and couldn't change my mind. I tried bad-mouthin her ever' chance I got fer the past two months, hopin' tuh git her outa my head. No fuckin luck at all. I love her more 'n ever. Jesus Christ!" He looked gloomily at the floor. "I figgered marryin' what's her name, Joyce, maybe I'd git over Mrs. Swift is all. Hell's bells!"

We sat a few minutes in silence, Buddy finishing his cigarette and sipping a glass of pink punch, me sipping the last of my coffee.

"So what about this ex-husband of hers?" I asked again. "What the hell became of him anyway?"

"Shit, he's out o' the picture except in her mind." He paused and looked angrily at the floor.

"Real sweet, sensitive son-of-a-bitch, I'd say about him," he went on grimly. "She claims he was jus' so sensitive he couldn't stand the sight of her shrunken leg. Christ, what bull shit!" Buddy leaned back and lit a Lucky Strike.

Suddenly, he leaned forward again, a curl of cigarette smoke trailing from his nose. He looked at me intensely. "See, that's what I mean about love," he said. "She really loved him, so she makes excuses for him, even when he's a total shithead. Christ, she'd take him back, I bet, if he happened to show up tomorrow—or next week. Goddam, she must be still in love with him, I s'pose, and that's why she won't even give me the time o' day."

"Did you ask her," I said, hopefully, thinking that if he could tie up with Stephanie, that might leave an opening in Joyce's life for someone who obviously loved her a lot more than Buddy did. "Just ask her right out how she feels about you," I suggested.

"Hell, no, I didn't ask her," he answered with harsh intensity and a certain note of sadness—or maybe despair. "But I could tell how she felt about me. She liked me all right cuz I was someone who would sit and listen to her and keep her company. She's lonely as hell out there all alone fer months at a time in winter at that damn school. She told me she even thought about killing herself when she had her accident, and then her husband dumped a ration o' shit all over her right after. She had to sign the goddam divorce papers when she was still in traction in the hospital, for Chrissake. Real sweet son-of-a-bitch, her husband. This here Marine would knock the piss outa him if I ever ran into him, by God."

"I suppose you knockin' the piss out of her ex-husband would suddenly make her fall for you. 'Oh, sweetheart, you knocked the piss outa my ex-old man. So now, I really do love you, after all.' Get a life," I said mockingly. "'Methinks, the fuckin' Marine deceiveth himself.'"

Ignoring me, Buddy went on, "So she went back to college, where she's now about to be a junior or somethin'. And when she got a chance at this job, she applies for a provisional teaching certificate and grabs it, and moves to the fuckin' backwater of the world. She said she hadn't even seen Burnham School when she signed the contract to teach there. Christ, she probably wouldn't o' come if she'd really seen the place."

He paused and took a light sip of beer. "She came, she met me, and away we go...and the rest is fuckin' history, as they say."

He paused again and changed the subject.

"Joyce, for Christsake, never wears a bra! I'm gonna have to talk to her about that. Jesus Christ!" He looked stern.

"Christ, you're repeating yourself," I told him. "How am I s'posed to learn anything if you just repeat yourself?"

"Well, I s'pose you know what a bra is, Mr. voice of experience. They're what you get rid of during the first step to makin' out. That was the first thing that got me with Joyce. No fuckin' bra. Real handy!" he added, smirking at me.

"You're so full of shit," I said. "First, you want Joyce to wear a bra, then you say it's handier without one. Which is it, Mr. Smart-ass, Know-it-all?"

"Well, when I'm gone, I don't want it to be too handy fer any other son-of-a-bitch," he said with a leer at me. "...like you if it comes to that." He took another sip of beer and went on with his story.

"And kids'll put a crease in a bitch's belly, too. More than one or two, if it comes to that. Creases, that is! Joyce's had two kids, yuh know, two that she's laid claim to anyways. I don't know how ever many more she might o' had. But Stephanie, by God, she's trim as a goddam Olympic runner, trim as a Greek goddess."

"Okay, okay," I said, "I believe you're head over heels in fuckin' love. Now, what the fuck are you gonna do about it? Marry Joyce, who you don't love, instead of Stephanie, who you do love." What about you goin' and askin' Stephanie to marry you or wait for you or something—instead of marryin' Joyce?" I asked hopefully.

"Hell, no, I couldn't do it," he said firmly. "I agreed to marry damn Joyce now, and Stephanie ain't gonna give me the time o' day, anyways. Even though she thinks I'm fuckin' artistic, right? Artists are s'posed to be sensitive, ain't they? And she thinks I got artistic talent and that shit. That's why she got me to git into this sign-painting school in the army. 'It'll teach you technique and discipline,' she says. Shit, I'd like to show her a little technique and discipline on various parts of her nude anatomy. I should ask her to pose in the nude, eh? Fer my future development as an artist and all that shit. She should be delighted to pose for the future, fuckin', sensitive artist, right?"

"Well, hell," I said, standing up and setting my empty coffee cut on the bar. "Good luck, anyway! I'm worn out as shit from gettin' hung up at the river last night so I'm gonna head on back to the school." I looked at Buddy quietly for a moment. "I'll tell Mrs. Swift you send her a goodbye. She asked after you when you didn't stop last night."

"Hell, no, don't say a word to her about me." He paused, then he looked at me sharply. "What else did she say about me?" He asked hopefully.

"Not a damn thing I remember," I said.

"I s'pose not," he said morosely.

"Well, see yuh, take it easy in the Marine Corps," I said.

"Yeah, okay," he said. In gloomy despair, he raised his hand to wave half-heartedly. "Don't you fergit to check on Joyce and the kids now while I'm pertectin' all yer asses in Hawaii."

"Okay by me," I said.

I had a chance to follow his orders on Joyce the minute I stepped through the door into the kitchen once again. She was sitting at the same table I had had coffee at earlier, sipping her own coffee and puffing angrily on a cigarette.

"Jesus Christ, what's holdin' him?" She asked. "Grouchy young smart-ass," she added.

"He should be along any minute. He ain't feelin' so hot about his dad kickin' him outa the house. He was just smokin' a cigarette and havin' a little more punch," I explained, feeling a need to smooth over the way Buddy had acted towards her.

"That's no damn excuse for him acting like such a prick," she said, fiercely stamping out her cigarette and reaching for another to light.

"Well, Goodbye," I said, sliding by her table shyly. I couldn't bring myself to look at her, afraid I wouldn't be able to help myself from staring longingly.

"Christ, you two must have had a lot of old times to talk over. Jesus Christ, it's takin' him forever. I ain't waitin' fer him very damn much longer." She stubbed out her new cigarette and threw the barely smoked butt on the floor. "Oh, hell, I'll walk you to the barn, if Mr. Smartass isn't going to get his ass in gear," she said, taking my arm and leading me through the door.

We walked across the dirty parking lot and stopped just in front of the stable door. Even in her pink high heels and the dress jacket on over her party skirt, she looked right at home in the stable.

"My God, is that your horse," Joyce asked, spotting Yellow Dab through the open upper half of the stable door. "He's really damn beautiful!" Yellow Dab perked up his ears as if he understood the compliment.

Joyce stepped ahead of me through the stable door. I tried to veil my stare but, when she stepped ahead of me and I was momentarily out of her line of sight, I couldn't take my eyes off the elegant way she moved and the graceful way she extracted another cigarette and was about to light it.

I reached out to take the lighter and hold it to the end of her cigarette, as I'd seen my dad do. He never had a lighter because he would only carry stick matches. My hand was shaking so hard I could hardly hold the match still. She cupped both her hands gently around my hand and directed the flame to her cigarette.

"Jesus Christ," she said in surprise, "your hand is freezing like ice and you look absolutely exhausted. What happened to you anyway? You look like hammered shit."

She held her cigarette daintily between her lips. "You don't smoke yet, do you?" she asked, offering me a puff. I shook my head.

She moved the cigarette between her teeth so she had both hands free. Lowering the zipper on her coat a bit, she took one of my hands in both of hers and rubbed it briskly, then tucked my fingers under her armpit. "You need to get those hands warm before they freeze," she said, patting my cheek, as she used to do when I'd been tagging along with my dad in the bars.

The palm of my hand cupped the outside of her breast. I could definitely feel she wasn't wearing any bra. She took my other hand in both of hers and tucked it under her other armpit. From the angle I was standing to her, the palm of that hand cupped nearly half her other breast, and I could feel her large nipple probing gently against my wrist.

"That should warm your frosty hands," she said comfortably, taking another drag on her cigarette. "Maybe, it will warm more than your hands," she added with an impish smile, not taking her eyes off mine. I found myself transfixed in a kind of ecstasy. Wild horses couldn't have dragged my eyes from her, nor my hands out of her armpits.

Chapter 11

COMPLICATIONS

"Christ, you must've got frozen clear to the bone," Joyce said after a few minutes, as she stubbed out her cigarette. "Your hands are still like icicles. We can't stand here all day while they warm up." She took my hands from her armpits and held them between her own hands.

"C'mon," she said, "follow me. I'll unveil the mysteries of this particular place for you." She drew me by the hand to a door at the back of the stable. "There's a granary back here with four grain bins." She stepped aside so she could show me inside the door. A narrow aisle passed down the middle of the room. On each side of the aisle were two large closed doors, made of clapboard, typical granary doors.

"You got a coupla blankets in that bedroll I saw tied behind your saddle?" she asked. "Grab 'em and follow me back here. We'll get you warmed up, or die tryin'"

I grabbed my bedroll and followed her down the aisle. She stopped at the last door. "Close that door and push that latch so it's locked," she told me.

In the gloom that followed closing the door, I almost ran into her as I went down the aisle to join her.

"You're gonna be surprised by this," she said, opening the last door leading to one of the grain bins. I followed inside and looked around in amazement. The inside of the grain bin had been transformed into a small bedroom, with a tiny square window in the wall where the grain door for throwing grain into the bin would ordinarily have been.

There was a bed tucked against one wall and a small propane heater and a chair opposite it. "Here, loan me a hand and I'll get this heater rollin'. It takes about two minutes to get warm as toast in here," she said, as she kneeled down in front of the heater and removed the face panel. She hitched her skirt up over her knees so it wouldn't touch the dusty floor. I had seen her legs often enough before, but looking down on her from my vantage point standing above her, she seemed totally vulnerable, like a little girl playing, totally indifferent to the modesty of keeping her skirt down. I felt an overwhelming need to protect her.

Suddenly, the blue flame whished alive in the heater, and Joyce replaced the face panel.

"Christ, I wish that old bastard would sweep this place once in awhile," she said, dusting her skirt and brushing her hands together. "Here, I'll give you a hand spreading your blankets." She helped me open my bedroll and spread the blankets and the covering tarp on the bed.

"Come on," she said, sitting on the edge of the bed. "Sit here beside me and we'll get those icicles you call hands warmed up in a minute."

Meekly, I sat down beside her and turned in her direction. She unzipped her coat and slipped it off but kept it draped over her shoulders. "See, I told you it warmed up in here in no time," she said.

She quickly pulled up her white sweater and tucked it under her breasts. "Okay, mister, get those hands in here," she said to me in what was almost a motherly tone. She took my one hand and tucked it under her sweater and into her cosy armpit, then followed suit with my other hand. "There, that should warm 'em up a little faster. My, but they're cold." She winced at the touch of my hands against her bare skin.

"You really don't wear a bra," I blurted out without thinking.

"Jeez, I didn't think you'd notice," she said teasingly. She cupped my cheeks with her long fingers and smiled at me. "So that's what you and Buddy were talkin' about so long in the bar there. About what I wear or don't wear, eh? I s'pose Buddy wants me to start wearin' a bra."

I hung my head guiltily, and nodded. "Please don't tell him I told you," I said, ashamed at breaking the confidence.

"Don't worry about that," she said and then added firmly, "and don't think I'm gonna start wearin' a bra either. We may get married, but that bossy little bastard ain't gonna start tellin' me what to do. Especially when the little bastard is leavin' for the Marine Corps in less than a week. I s'pose he figures I should wait in Bull Hook, Montana, for him. That boring fucking hole. And I'm s'posed to wait for him with bated breath and a bra on." She was building up quite a head of steam when she stopped and smiled at me. "No fuckin' way is he gonna boss me around. Not on your life," she added firmly, "he ain't gonna change me or my life one damn bit. I wouldn't change a hair on my head for him," she smiled at me, "unless he asked me damn nicely, that is." She scrubbed her fingers around on my cheeks and walked them to the back of my neck where she clamped them gently around my head to keep me facing her.

"You wouldn't ever ask me to change my life, would you, Little Lew?" She brushed her lips along the side of my neck, then across my cheek and finally settled them for a moment on my mouth.

"Christ," she said, pulling back away from me for a bit but not so far I couldn't keep my hands warming under her armpits. She pulled her sweater up over her large breasts and put her hands under them, lifting the nipples towards me. "Jesus, you tell me if you think I need to wear a bra," she said.

"No, no," I murmured in a strangled voice, unable to remove my eyes from her large red nipples set against the warm brown circles that surrounded them.

"Christ, men think they own the goddamed world. Well, that's damn well gonna change. No man's gonna damn well boss me around…without a discussion, at least," she said, pulling her sweater over her head and tossing it aside. "See, I told you," she added. "It gets warm as hell in here in about two minutes."

I thought she was getting uncomfortable, so I started gently to extract my hands from her armpits.

"No, leave them there," she said in a considerate tone. "Your hands get warm a lot faster there than they would even in a warm room."

"That fat old bastard," she continued, "MacElroony or MacElroy or whatever, the sick old pervert that runs this bar, showed me this room one night when he thought some friends of mine had left me here. He thought I'd put out for him or something, I guess, if he let me sleep in here. Fat chance, the sick ol' fart. I bet the old bastard has nothin' good to say about me since that time, anyway. Good thing my friends came back just in time and picked me up, or I might have had to club the old bastard to keep him off me. He's a strong old son-of-a-bitch on top of it all, hoistin' those damn heavy beer kegs around all the time, and shit like that.

"He tells me he comes back here to sleep when there gets to be too many fights in the bar. He hides out here and locks himself in 'til the drunks go home or settle down or whatever. Then, he comes out and kicks their asses into the snow drift if they're passed out in the bar. Since then, I've slept jags off here whenever I feel like it and he's never bothered me since that one time." She removed my hands and stood up so she could throw my tarp off the bed and lay back on my top blanket that was underneath it. She undid the buttons on the side of her dance skirt and dropped it carefully so it wouldn't touch the floor. She hung it and her sweater on two of several nails in the wall that served as clothes hooks. "See, I do wear panties and panty hose, anyway," she added. She pulled the panty hose down her thighs and sat back down on the bed.

"He did say some bad things about you when I first got here," I admitted to her. "But I didn't believe a damn word he said," I added firmly.

"Hell, you're so damn sweet, Little Lew," she said. "Here, let's get more comfortable and we'll finish warming you up." She bent over and undid the straps across the tops of her pink shoes. After dropping them to the floor, she bounced herself back onto the bed and dug her dainty toes under the edge of my leg.

"Come on," she said, "get a few of those dingy wet clothes off...and pull off your boots. I need a nap after that damnable Buddy woke me so early this morning. So you can lie with me awhile and finish warmin' up." She was sitting partially reclined at the head of the bed with only her nearly transparent panties left on. She clearly liked my abject adoration and arched her back a bit to set off her figure. She had one leg draped gracefully across the other to hide all but just a peek at the top fringe of her pubic hair.

"God," I said to myself with a guilty twinge. "Her breasts do appear to sag a little bit, just like Buddy said. "But they're even more beautiful that way," I added to myself, with loyalty for my complete devotion to Joyce. I recalled Buddy's remark that the sign of true love is to defend even the loved ones most obvious faults. "By God, they're totally beautiful and don't let that bastard Buddy say anything about them again, or I'd deck him." Just as that was running through my mind, I noticed the faint white lines of stretch marks across her stomach and felt another pang of guilt and disloyalty for even noticing.

"Wow, interesting by comparison," I thought to myself, recalling Buddy's story of his quick glance at Mrs. Swift's nakedness. She had been completely naked and hadn't even made an effort to conceal her pubic triangle. Joyce had uncovered herself voluntarily, but she was holding back just the last glimpse of her pubis with an alluring smile and a teasing manner. I tried to avoid thinking about it and tried more or less successfully to keep from staring at her partially covered crotch.

When I bent over and attempted to get my boots off, I couldn't get them to budge. I was almost crying at the pain pulling on my boots caused.

"What's wrong, Lew?" Joyce, asked with concern. She sat up behind me with her arms resting gently on my shoulders while I tried unsuccessfully to dislodge my boots. "You must have frozen your feet and they're a little swollen." She jumped off the bed, unconcerned about her bare feet and the rough boards on the floor.

"Here, let me try," she said. She reached down and lifted my right leg from the floor. She swung her one leg over, so she was straddling my leg, the shadowy crack of her ass resting firmly against my leg, where I could faintly detect it through her panties.

"Help me, now," she said, putting both of her hands under the heel of my boot and giving a abrupt jerk. Amazingly, the boot slipped off with no trouble. I reached down and pulled off my heavy wool sock, shocked to discover it was soaking wet again and I couldn't even remember how it had happened.

"Jesus, your foot's a mess," she said, picking it up to pat it gently. "Where are my damn glasses when I need 'em?" She put my foot down briefly, then retrieved her glasses to inspect my foot more closely.

"Well, it looks okay," she gave her verdict. "It's just bruised and swollen, no gray flesh that might be trouble. Rest it for half and hour or so here without that boot on and the swelling will go down a little and it'll be okay. But, be damn careful you don't freeze it again for the next coupla weeks or so." She patted my foot playfully and set it down.

"We better get this one, too," she continued. She straddled my other leg and extracted that boot just as easily. She set both boots near the stove to dry and hung my two wet socks on nails over the stove, where they also would dry. She bounced back into the bed and pulled the blanket up to her chin, but still kept an eye on my progress.

"Now, get those sorry wet pants off and that shirt and hop into bed with me here, so I can really warm you up, and send you on your way in a little better shape than you presented yourself to me." She sounded very much like my mother as she said that. My mother always patted me on my cheek when she asked me to do something in her gentle but insistent voice.

I pulled off the wet pants and the shirt, which at least was dry, and stood shivering forlornly beside the bed in my shorts, which I realized were also somewhat wet. "Come on in," Joyce said, pulling the covers aside and gesturing to me. "We'll get you under the covers and have you warmed up in no time. See I told you that little gas heater warmed it up in here in nearly no time at all."

I crawled into the bed carefully and stretched out without touching Joyce. My feet felt so much better I could almost have cried over that.

"How's the feet?" Joyce asked with genuine concern. She leaned on her elbow and looked down at me where I was lying stiffly under my blanket. I was wondering what I would do if she touched me or grabbed me or something. "You look like you're about to be crucified," she added, patting my cheeks and giving me a quick kiss on the forehead.

"My feet feel lots better," I managed to say feebly. "Thanks for getting my boots off." I glanced at her with grateful appreciation, wondering if I should give her a quick kiss by way of thanks. "I don't know if I'da been able to get 'em off without your help or not," I added pathetically. Even in the warm room under the wool Hudson's Bay blanket from my bedroll, I couldn't stop shivering.

"Jeez, Little Lew," she said to me, "you're the sweetest goddam kid I know. Saints be praised if you're not. My God, I'd love to have you for my very own. Steal you from your mother and that damn rambunctious old man o' yours." She gave me a gentle kiss on the cheek and slid one of her arms under my neck and let the other rest softly on my chest." She paused thoughtfully, "Christ, your old man is a real pistol if there ever was one. Mostly, he's almost as sweet as you," she added, pinching one of the nipples of my chest, causing me to take in a quick breath. "But, God, he's got the worst goddam temper. He blows his stack, kicks every dog or girl in sight. Then, in two minutes, he's fine again. God, I really like your dad, even though I'm pretty mad at him here lately. And for a while more than lately, if it comes to that."

She snuggled her bosom against my side and moved her hips and thighs against the ramrod posture I couldn't avoid maintaining, even as I continued to shiver.

"God, you're cold as ice all over," she said. "You're shiverin' to beat hell, and your goddam shorts are even soakin' wet. Goddam, what the hell happened to you anyway?"

"Me and my horse fell off the road allowance when it washed out last night," I admitted hesitantly, afraid she might think badly of me for being stupid and trying to cross the flooded road grade. "The road was okay when we started across," I added hastily by way of explanation. "Then, my God, it washed out right under Yellow Dab's feet, and we washed down towards the reservoir, until we could get swum out."

"Christ, so's yer stuck on the other side of that coulee, where there's nobody lives for twenty miles, except across the river where yer folks got their place. I s'pose you ain't had yer clothes off since then either, to get 'em properly dried."

"No, I stopped at Lucien DuMont's place for a minute and caught a nap. But then I went on, and I guess I stayed pretty wet," I admitted.

"Jesus Christ, your shit-headed dad should have his head examined for having you riding around the country in the spring, when the goddam ice is breaking up and all the streams are runnin' bank full or more," she said with an accusing tone. Then she added somewhat forgivingly, "God help us all be better parents."

"I can take care of myself okay," I answered her. I didn't want her to think of me as a kid. "Yellow Dab just couldn't do anything when the flood washed out the road. Usually he takes care of me real well. He's a real good horse."

She was reacting very differently than I thought she would. I figured she would blame me for being stupid, as my dad would do, I felt sure. But she blamed my dad. I'd never even thought of the situation in that way before.

"He's a beauty, all right," she said. "I don't know when I've seen a prettier horse."

"I picked him out when he was just a colt and broke him to lead and ride myself. Dad said he's give me a horse if I'd learn to take care of it and break it myself and everything," I said enthusiastically, remembering the joys of horse-breaking. "Since then, I broke lots o' horses," I paused, not wanting to brag. "Good ones, too, only I wish Dad hadn't sold every damn one of those other horses I broke—except for Yellow Dab and a pretty little bay gelding that I named Kidd after Captain Kidd. He gave me a bunch of horses and took 'em all back and sold 'em as soon as I got 'em broke. But he did let me keep those two." I could feel that I was beginning to relax, as she let me talk. "They were my two favorites, anyway," I added, sorry I'd implied a criticism of my dad.

"Oh, shit," she said suddenly, jumping out of the bed and tossing the cover back. "Damn, I didn't inspect your other foot to make sure it's okay. Christ, remember that stupid son-of-a-bitch working down at the Bull Hook Livestock there. Froze his damn feet and kept walkin' on 'em 'cause they quit hurtin' after they were froze. Then, he comes into the office and inspects only one of 'em and figures he's okay. Shit, he gets gangrene in the other one. We had to cut his shoe off, and son-of-a-bitch if they didn't have to cut off his foot at the hospital. Amputated the damn thing right below the knee. Jeez, I dunno if you were workin' down there with your dad when that happened." She inspected both of my feet carefully, lighting a match in the gloom of the room to make sure both were okay. The light of the match glowed on the tops of her breasts, where they swayed eerily over my two bare feet, as she bent over to inspect them. "God, she's absolutely and thoroughly beautiful," I said to myself, with a lump of sorrow in my throat since my long-term chances with her still didn't look too good. "But the short term chances are doing good," I thought with a smile, thinking that her naked body with the thin covering at the crotch looked as much like the picture of the statue of Athena from Athens that was printed in an encyclopedia at school as anything else I'd ever seen.

"Well, they look good to me," she said, "just bruised and swollen. And the swelling's even going down after you got them damn tight boots off." She patted my feet with her hands and raised her head to look at me. "My, your legs are getting pretty hairy. Maybe, it'll grow a little more on your chest later." She patted the calves of my legs. I pulled the blanket back over my naked chest. "Three black hairs, at best," I thought, glancing down at my chest as I quickly covered it, "and a lot of damn peach fuzz."

"And what's more, Mr. Shy Guy," she added, snagging my shorts and dragging them off over my feet, "we're gonna take off those sopping wet shorts and hang them up to dry. Winter time still, and you're wearing shorts instead of long johns. That's not too damn smart for a smart kid, used to country livin'."

I dragged the blanket over my waist and feet to cover my sudden nakedness. I didn't know whether to protest her abrupt action or not. "I figured winter was over," I said, defensively.

"Well, you can't depend on the weather in Montana fer shit," she said. "Hot one day and freezin' yer ass the next. You should know. You been in Montana all your life, haven't you?" She tossed the blanket back with complete unconcern for my nakedness and crawled across me to lie down on her side of the bed. She tossed the blanket over me and drew it up to her neck with a shiver.

"Real nice blanket," she said, "but not enough to get me warm very quickly. Now, I've been workin' to warm you up, so's you're gonna have to give me a hand as well. Shit, it's cold out there with no clothes, even with that damn little heater on." She rolled on her side towards me. "C'mon now," she went on, "up on your side facing me. You're gonna have to snuggle me 'til I get warm, like it er not." She enfolded me in her arms and I instinctively put my arms around her and held her gently against myself, wondering what the hell I should do next—if I dared do anything at all.

Chapter 12

FRUSTRATIONS AND MORE

I lay quietly next to her, slowly beginning to relax. I was glad she ignored my erection. 'Hard-on' was the term I was used to, but I had learned the more polite term in something I had read, so out of deference to my overwhelming and somewhat distressing feelings for 'Joy' — as I now tended to refer to her to myself—I felt I should use the polite term, even to myself. I couldn't have done anything about my erection anyway, even if she'd said something derogatory about it because it definitely had a mind of its own. It lay at something of an angle along the top of her thigh. She had adjusted her position next to me a bit so there was room for it. Otherwise, she seemed to pay no attention.

She was rubbing her fingers up and down my back, so I began to do the same with her back. She showed her appreciation by sighing in my ear and letting a breath of warm air sweep gently along my neck behind my ear. The rush of warm air along my neck almost caused me to lose my studied calm completely. I stiffened up to regain control of myself.

"Don't you like that?" she asked with concern in her voice.

"No, I liked it a lot," I admitted, barely able to whisper.

"Jesus, an honest man! That's sure as hell a rarity," she whispered back to me. She rewarded me by moving her free hand along my rib cage, while she cupped her hand that was trapped under me around the cheek of my ass and squeezed gently.

She giggled a bit as she felt me instinctively thrust my pelvis forward. "You liked that okay, eh?" she asked.

I caught my breath and tried to answer but couldn't form any words.

"Here, let me show you something I like," she whispered in my ear. She took my free hand and held it in hers for a moment. Then, she inclined her torso away from me at a slight angle, allowing a breath of cool air to rush between us. "O-o-o, that fresh air feels great," she said with a sigh. She moved the hand of mine she had ahold of up her body until she held it cupped over her breast. She moved her hand on top of mine, so I was kneading her breast, with her help and guidance, of course.

"Like bread dough," I thought to myself, so I wouldn't go crazy with what I was doing. I remembered Mrs. Swift kneading the dough with which she had made cinnamon rolls for us when I'd stayed over at the school during the winter. That made me almost say her name 'Stephanie' aloud. "Wow, that would be pretty stupid," I thought to myself. "I didn't think even Joyce would be understanding enough to let it go if I said another girl's name at that precise time."

"Joy-y-y," I sighed instead, with a catch in my voice that I had not intended.

"Now, take it easy," Joyce said softly in my ear. "You're really too young anyway to go the whole way and have sex yet, but you can get an education and learn some stuff, now that you're graduated out of eighth grade. I'll show you a few things, so's you will know better what to do when the time comes. Is that okay with you?" she whispered to me.

"All right," I managed to sigh in her ear. I was a little disappointed that we weren't going "the whole way," as she put it. I was sure I was old enough to go ahead, but her promise to teach me a "few things" definitely caught my interest. Maybe, I was too young, as she said, but I'd at least know something about it—if the time ever came.

"Okay," she said to me softly, "let me show you something else that most girls really like—including me if you must know." She cupped her hand around the back of my hand that was covering her breast and moved that hand slowly across her stomach and up and down each side of her inner thighs, avoiding the target, where I thought I knew it had to be.

"Now, touch me very gently, right there," she said, holding my index finger and second finger together and brushing them gently over a noticeable protrusion that seemed to be just below her pubic hair.

"Gently, very gently," she repeated, "just massage your fingers back and forth and up and down over that little bump there. But very, very gently!" She relaxed and occasionally moaned softly against my neck as I kept up my task just as she had instructed me. "That's called the clit," she whispered breathlessly in my ear, "and it's really the center of response for girls…for most girls anyway."

She lay back and sighed occasionally with tremors sometimes causing her whole body to shudder. "Gently, very gently," she kept repeating, like a mantra I'd read about in Buddhism. Maybe, that was a Buddhist instruction in making love, I thought, very puzzled by the possibility. Religion may have its real foundation in sex after all, I thought…or in lack of sex, I considered, thinking of St. Paul and his hangups about sex. My poor Catholic mother would have been shocked at my thoughts. I smiled about it to myself.

"God," Joyce sighed in my ear, "I wish you were mine. My very own boy. You're not a know-it-all like that damn Buddy. He has sex one time before he met me with some whore in an alley, and based on that, he, for Chrissakes, thinks he knows it all. God, he's strictly 'slam-bam, thank you, ma'am,'…or is it 'slam-bang, thank you ma'am," she asked with a small giggle. "Anyway, that sure applies to him. He's got no control at all. No matter what I do, he's inside me and done in ten seconds. Then, he blames his frustration—and mine—on me. 'You oughta know what you're doin' to get satisfied,' he says. Fuck him, arrogant little fucker. I'd show him if he'd pay any attention, but being himself, of course, he thinks he knows it all. He won't pay any attention to me or listen to what I have to say."

"Christ, maybe I can talk to him," I whispered to her, feeling bad for both of them.

"No, no, I don't think that would do. Don't do that," she said urgently. She giggled. "He'd figure out for damned sure I said something to you if you tell him. He'd sure as hell be mad as hell about that."

"Okay," I agreed reluctantly, glad for the interruption of my arousal. Before it had happened, I was afraid I couldn't hold on much longer without doing something crazy that I'd be totally embarrassed about.

"Jesus," she sighed in my ear, "you really figure out fast what to do. But then you got a good teacher, too." She sighed again, her hips beginning to thrust forward and rotate, so it was harder to keep up my steady, gentle attention to her clit, as she had called it.

"God, slow down a minute. "You're almost drivin' me completely over the edge," she whispered. "God, you're so sweet, just like my own dear little baby," she added softly to me in a more normal tone of voice. She put both arms around my head and cradled it against her bosom for a minute, rocking back and forth. "My own sweet baby," she repeated.

"I think I'll have you nurse my teat like a baby," she went on, patting my head as if I were a baby. "You know, that's what I miss most about havin' my kids get older. I just loved it when I could rock their little heads back and forth, and they would grab onto my nipple for dear life, and nurse to their little heart's content. Jesus Christ, that's almost the best feeling I've ever had in my entire life, including sex with a damn man and everything else."

She patted my cheeks and lifted my head above her nearest breast. "Okay, open up, little one, my baby." She pushed my cheeks until I instinctively opened my mouth. I let her draw my mouth over her large nipple and without thinking I began to nurse like a baby. "Oh, God, open your mouth, my sweet baby. Open your mouth wide, wide, and nurse hard as you can, my sweet one. Oh, God, that feels great!"

Without thinking about it, I realized that I was in a good position to massage her clit again. I gently ran my free hand up her thigh and tentatively massaged the little bump that the apex of her pubic hair pointed towards.

Before I realized what was happening, she grabbed my hand in both of hers and jammed it against the opening just below her clit. Her hips arched up, lifting me with them, as if I were balanced on an arched bridge, and a scream ripped from her mouth that almost frightened me into flight.

"Oh, God! Oh, God! O, God! ...," she kept repeating. Her two hands holding mine plunged my hand time and again against her orifice. I suddenly had an epiphany that made me think I knew what she wanted. I shaped my fingers as I had when I had plunged them in to examine the lamb in the ewe's womb.

She next time she slammed my hand against her crotch, it plunged inside her, not terribly gently, I realized. She stiffened and her whole torso seemed to erupt off the bed towards the ceiling.

"Oh, my God," she screamed again, "get it out of me." But both of her hands had a death-grip on my arm. Her grip had me positively locked inside of her. She rocked up towards the ceiling, with her back arched so much I had to slide off her and release her nipple from my mouth. Her prolonged scream almost scared me out of the room. I must have hurt her really bad, I thought dismally.

"Christ," she said, relaxing a bit, and gently drawing my hand from inside her. "Where the hell did you learn to do that?" she asked.

Since I thought I had hurt her, I didn't want to say. "Well," I whispered reluctantly, "it's how I learned to shape my hand to reach inside a sheep—or sometimes even a cow—to see if the lamb can come through between the ewe's pelvic bones."

"Well, it sure as hell works great," she said. "I s'pose you learned how to do that from your old man. Funny," she giggled, "I guess you outfoxed him because I bet he never used that grip on a woman. Not on me, anyway...," she caught herself and stopped speaking. I sat up abruptly and jerked away from her. My penis shrank as if I'd been shot.

"God, I'm sorry," she said. "I didn't ever mean to tell you, but your dad and I did have sex a few times...while you were at the movies and stuff. But you're much gentler than he is. You'll sure as hell be a better lover." I guess she thought I was jealous but, of course, that wasn't it at all.

When she said what she did, I could only think of my poor mother, sitting at home alone, waiting for us, while I sipped tea and read Hemingway, and my dad fucked the woman I now loved more uncontrollably than ever before. I felt a rage of fury towards my dad, but my fury didn't touch Joyce.

I didn't even think about blaming her until she said, "I'm just awful damned sorry. I was a blabber-mouthed fool to say anything to you. Please don't blame me! I couldn't stand it if you held it against me!"

"I don't blame you at all," I said. "I didn't even think about it.

It's my goddam dad that's to blame."

"Now, don't blame him too much, either," Joyce said. "Don't be too hard on him. Men, most men anyway, are just like that, you know. Maybe, you can take this lesson to heart and learn to be better than some other men." She clutched her arms around me tightly and rocked me back and forth. "That would be a good outcome for all this, anyway," she whispered in my ear.

I was silent but vowed I would never do what my dad had done to betray my mother. Even more deeply in my heart, I vowed I would get some ultimate revenge on my dad. "That son-of-a-bitch," I said aloud in a fierce tone."

"Now, now," Joyce said, "don't go off feelin' that way about your dad. He really is a great guy! A little crazy and bad-tempered sometimes, but a great guy."

"I'll never forget and I'll never forgive him," I said with hard menace in my voice.

She rocked me back and forth in her arms until I calmed down. "One thing, maybe," she said, "you seem to have a bad temper, a little like your dad's. I never even saw him erupt as bad as you just did about him. You better learn to hang onto your temper a little bit better than he does. It's caused him a lot of trouble in his life already, that's for sure."

"I hope it causes him a lot more," I said, but I had pretty well become resigned to the fact that my dad had betrayed my mother—probably hundreds of times, if it came to that. I laughed a bit stiffly. "I s'pose I'm really just jealous... because he did it with you," I admitted.

"That's sweet of you to say," she said, patting my head once again, where it rested against her naked bosom.

She kept rocking my head back and forth as we lay back on the bed.

"You know, I've never really had that happen to me before," she said, contemplatively. "I always figured, all these years, that I couldn't have an orgasm without a cock inside me because of what my step-dad did to me when I was a kid." She paused, reflectively. "Well, I guess you proved me wrong on that score," she added, "because, my God, if that wasn't a real orgasm, goddam it, I'll eat a pig…or bite a hole outa his ass tryin', anyway. You really caught me by surprise there…with your little maneuver. That musta been what pushed me over," she said. "But you didn't have to tell me you learned it with a sheep," she added, laughing. "Fuckin' sheep is s'posed to be for old fuckers, like old sheep herders and the fuckin' dirty son-of-a-bitch that was my step-father. I can't imagine why my mother ever married the dirty, low-life ol' sheep-fucker, anyway. He diddled me from the time I was about six until I was sixteen and could get to hell outa the house and be on my own."

"Maybe, you should forgive and forget about him, too, like you told me to do with my dad. Maybe, you'd feel better about it," I said earnestly.

"Maybe the moon is made of green cheese, too," she said fiercely. "The dirty old bastard," she added and started to cry convulsively.

At that, I put my arms around her and tried to console her.

"You're such a sweet boy," she sniffled. "You've got to come by and see me every chance you get in my little house in town, where I live with my kids…and with my new husband, fuckin' Buddy, for a few days anyway, if we really go through with it."

We held each other a bit longer, and then she pushed me away. "We didn't do much for you this time around, did we," she said, tweaking my supine penis between her fingers. Maybe, we can do better by you next time. I think it's better if you get a little older, anyway. Next, I'll be accused of molesting kids. I sure as hell don't need that." She kissed me gently on the forehead.

"You better get dressed and get out of here," she continued even more earnestly. You can come by my house as soon as you can now, but if somebody should come lookin' and find us here, I don't know what awful stories might be makin' the rounds. You still look too much like a kid for word to get around about us. Besides, it would really piss your dad off if he ever found out."

Her comment gave me a perfect idea for how I would work some revenge on my dad. Somehow, I'd start visiting Joyce as often as I could, and then let him find out about it, somehow. "I'll think about it and work out the details later," I thought to myself.

I kissed her firmly on the mouth, then jumped out of bed and started quickly to get dressed. It all went well until I came to my boots, but I managed to get them on as well, without too much trouble. The swelling of my feet had definitely gone down some with my boots off.

When I was all dressed, I kneeled on the bed and pulled Joyce into my arms again. We held each other for what seemed like a long while, her almost entirely naked with just her filmy panties on, and me, now fully dressed and ready to move.

"I gotta get a nap," she said finally. "I'm completely frazzled after the party last night…and then this morning with you.…"

"I better get down to the school anyway," I said, "in case my dad shows up." I guess I added the last from force of habit. I didn't really give a goddam if he showed up or not. I was determined to make my own decisions and not listen to him from then on in.

"You all be sure to come and see me just as soon as you can," Joyce said, letting me out at the door and then pushing the latch back into place.

When I led Yellow Dab out of the barn, I ran into Buddy coming out the backdoor of the bar. "What the hell you still doin' here?" he asked. "I thought you was on yer way long since."

"I was just currying the nag and letting him eat some oats," I lied blandly.

"Where's that goddam bitch, Joyce? I s'pose the dirty cunt run off somewhere, pissed off at me about what I said," he said, mournfully.

"I sure as hell would be pissed off at what you said," I told him, laughing my ass off to myself. "You better apologize to beat hell at the way you treated her when you see her again. Maybe, she'll forgive you, but I sure as hell wouldn't."

"Yeah, yer right," Buddy said miserably.

"When I saw her in the bar, she said she was goin' back in the bar or someplace and grab a nap," I said. "See you later, cannon-fodder," I added. "I'll see you after you and the other damn jar-heads have massacred the Russkies and the Chinese…and brought the Philippines back into the union as a state. That'll be fuckin' never, man, you can depend on it."

"Yeah, so long, classmate," he said, smiling at me. "If you wise up and join the elite corps, maybe we can have chow someplace where they serve better food than the dog shit you git here in Montana."

I waved as I rode Yellow Dab around the corner of the bar. I didn't laugh until I had crossed Highway 2, but then I let go and I couldn't stop laughing.

Chapter 13

APPRENTICESHIP OF THE TRICKSTER

"The Trickster strikes again," I shouted, as I laughed my way down the county road that led to Lucien DuMont's place and that branched off a few miles ahead to cross Fresno Dam, which dammed up the Milk 'n Honey River and backed up a big irrigation reservoir that supplied irrigation water to the river valley through the dry summers.

"The Apprenticeship of the Trickster," I said more softly to Yellow Dab. "I'm apprenticing to be the Trickster and you, my big beautiful, off-color yellow cayuse, are my shaman's pony, carrying me on my way to insight and adventure." When I was a kid, I had loved my Grandfather's stories of the Cree Trickster, Wi-tsak-i-tsak, who tricked people and had many adventures in the old stories of the Cree.

I had always identified with Wi-tsak-i-tsak and thought I wanted to grow up and have adventures and escapades like his. Although none of the stories seemed to be about W-tsak-i-tsak as a child, I always thought he had to have a childhood when he somehow learned to be a Trickster. I wanted to know the story of that childhood. I wanted to model myself after that Trickster childhood, to be a Trickster myself, the Apprenticeship of the Trickster.

When I asked my Grandfather about the stories of the childhood of the Trickster, he always smiled and put me off. One day, when I was particularly insistent, he said to me mysteriously with the gentle protective smile he always turned on me, "You don't need to hear those stories of Trickster's childhood, because you're already livin' those stories yourself." As was my Grandfather's way, he wouldn't repeat what he said or explain what he meant.

But now as I turned onto the county road heading east towards Burnham School, I glanced at the mid-morning Sun that was halfway through its morning journey, and I thought of my Grandfather's words again. "By God, maybe he meant that I was destined to be a Trickster," I said to Yellow Dab, "and then you would be my shaman's pony, indeed." I hadn't ever thought of my Grandfather's remark in that particular way before.

"Maybe, he meant that I didn't have to hear the stories of the childhood of the Trickster because I was living that childhood myself in my own life," I said inquiringly to Yellow Dab. Yellow Dab whinnied gently and turned his ears sharply forward. "God, maybe he's understood me and is answering," I thought with a certain vague awe at the mysteries of the world that we as humans knew so little about, especially the totally alien world of animals and other so-called lowly creatures.

"But, boy," I said to him, patting his shoulder, "maybe Grandfather just meant that most childhoods are alike and will prepare you for whatever you want to be in the future—if you try and work hard enough to be what you want to be." I couldn't think what else I might want to be in this life, but I was dead sure I wanted to live the life of a Trickster, whatever that might involve.

Yellow Dab whinnied softly again, and I realized with a little embarrassment that he was not answering me, as I had for a breathless moment thought he was. Instead, he had seen something across the field off the road and was trying to call my attention to it.

There was a little draw running a full stream of snow water across the road. It would be no problem to cross, but it wasn't the draw itself that Yellow Dab had noticed. I pulled him to a stop and tried to follow his line of sight, where his ears pointed across the field towards a slight movement that I could now detect on the edge of the swiftly running little stream.

"Jesus Christ, I see it, too, boy," I told Yellow Dab, patting his neck, "but what the hell is it?" I could see the point where the movement had been but could detect no further movement. "Christ, I'm gonna check this out," I concluded to Yellow Dab.

"Shit, there's no damn way for you to get through that damned barbed wire fence," I told Yellow Dab, looking up and down the fence line that followed the county road. "We'd have to let down the fence to get you across." I hopped off Yellow Dab's back, my feet now feeling considerably better, and led Yellow Dab forward to examine the fence line.

"Hell, it's double stapled," I reported to Yellow Dab. "It'd be too damn much trouble to let it down.

"What the hell!" I continued, "it's only a little damn way over to where that movement was. You stay here and I'll walk over and see if I can spot what it is." I patted Yellow Dab's neck so he would know I wasn't leaving for long. After looping his reins around a post, I started walking through the mud across the field.

"Jeez, what a soggy mess!" I called back to Yellow Dab. "You're lucky to be hangin' on the gravel road."

I slogged towards the spot where Yellow Dab and I had spotted the movement. Suddenly, I glimpsed what appeared to be the rounded top of the head of an animal with brilliant shining eyes peering over the bank of the stream at me, large ears flicking nervously.

"Jesus Christ," I said aloud to myself, "is that a little fox kitten or a wolf cub or what the hell is it, and why the hell isn't it following its animal instinct of fear for humans and running its ass outa here?"

The two yellow eyes continued to follow me, showing no fear but sending out a baleful warning to steer clear.

"Christ, you're a nervy little bastard," I said, a little concerned that he would attack me as I drew closer. "Maybe, the little son-of-a-bitch has rabies," I thought. But he showed no sign of moving away from his cover under the bank of the stream.

"What the hell are you doing there?" I asked him with genuine curiosity. As I drew closer still, I could see that he was nearly ready to be drowned. Only his head was lying on the bank above the surface of the stream, and the rest of his body was submerged underwater. Clearly, the rushing water was quickly sapping what little strength he had left and would soon carry him under to a wet grave.

"A watery grave is what it will be for you, my friend," I said, as I stood above him looking down at his predicament. He bared his fangs at me and hissed warningly. I could now tell he was a small coyote pup, far less than half grown, from an early spring litter.

"Why don't you just climb outa there?" I said to him softly. "You must be stuck on something under the damn water." I knelt beside him and tried to peer into the water swirling by him. "It's too damn muddy," I told him, conversationally. "I can't see a goddam thing in there."

"Are you gonna cooperate and be good and let me see what the hell's holdin' you under there?" I asked him, hopefully. I tried to reach over him into the water to feel what was holding him, but he bared his fangs and snapped at me threateningly.

"Shit, you tough little bastard," I said with some admiration, "you'd have a snack on a piece of my arm there if you had half a chance, even though I'm tryna save your ass from drowning." I stood up and looked down at him doubtfully.

"Damn you, are you worth the fuckin' trouble?" I asked him with trepidation. "Shit, I'm gonna have to get something to hold your damn head against the bank, then I'm gonna have to get goddam wet again to see what the hell's holding you underwater."

I retrieved a short rose bush branch that was waving above the running water. It's root was submerged, but I gritted my teeth and reached under the icy water, so I could get enough of the root to include where it was forked, as I knew it would be, just below the surface of the ground. It was easy to unearth because the water had already soaked the soil around it.

"Now, Mr. Coyote, see if you can take a nip out of me with that fork planted against your neck," I told the pup.

I walked just upstream of where he was and planted the forked root against his neck. He snapped fiercely to try to dislodge it but no luck. He had no strength left to put up a fight. Tentatively, I stepped into the rushing water with one foot, trying to find the bottom before I stepped in with my other foot.

"Christ almighty, that's cold," I shrieked, involuntarily. Worse yet, I couldn't find the bottom of the stream with my lead foot, so I had to step in with both feet. I slid down the slippery underwater bank of mud until I hit the bottom of the little draw, the force of the running water pushing against me almost knocking me off my feet.

"Goddam, that's deeper than I thought," I said. I could already feel the icy water in my boots. Once again, I almost lost my footing in the mud when I tried to draw a little closer to the pup. "Shit, that's all I need, to fall into this son-of-a-bitching spring bath," I said. I regained my feet, but the goddam stream was still whipping around my waist, and it was hard to keep my balance against the force of the water.

I felt under the water along the coyote's drenched body. When my exploration reached his rear thigh, I knew what his problem was.

"Shit," I said to him, "you poor little bugger, some bastard set a coyote trap and anchored it to the bottom of the draw. Before it became a torrent with snow melt," I said sympathetically to the little coyote, hoping he would understand that not all humans were out to get a bounty for his ears, or a couple of bucks for his hide. A little guy like him wouldn't have a hide worth much more. But the bounty paid off, no matter what the size of the coyote ears that were turned in.

"They ain't patrolling their trap-line for a few days because it's too goddam muddy," I went on with my commentary to the coyote. Or is it a soliloquy, I asked myself. "But you seem to be listening pretty close to me, don't you?" I said to the little coyote.

I knew he must be listening to the sound of my voice because he was clearly calming down. Or giving up, I thought. But either way he must be listening to me a little bit.

"You hear me okay, don't you?" I asked him, "But who the Christ knows what you understand me to mean?" I patted his head soothingly.

"So they leave you out here to drown, you poor little son-of-a-bitch," I said to him, hoping he'd understand. Myself, I hated all trappers although I trapped a little bit as well, occasionally through the winter months to make a few bucks. But, I thought, I patrol my damn trap-line twice a day because it was on the route I rode to school. In the spring, I pulled the traps because I couldn't patrol them properly.

I kicked the trap spring and released the jaws. I clamped one hand around the coyote pup's mouth to hold it closed while I struggled up the bank with him in my arms.

"You're one wet little bastard," I said, looking him over as I reached the top of the bank. "Christ, you tried to chew your leg off where it was in the goddam trap," I said, noticing teeth marks above where the jaws of the trap had cut into his thigh. "Hell, you'd never be able to chew through there," I told him. The jaws had closed too far up his thigh for him to have a chance of chewing his leg off.

"You tried anyway, you tough little bastard," I said, patting his head gently. Feeling my warmth, he now just huddled against me without response. "I s'pose the water came up too soon for you to do too much chewin' on yer leg anyway," I added, patting his head again. "You woulda drowned before you could get that damn leg chewed off at your thigh. Your thigh's just too big a bone to chew through, even for you, you sharp-toothed little bastard."

As I struggled through the mud back across the field, I saw a battered gray pickup pull up where Yellow Dab was tied to the fence. As I climbed through the fence and undid Yellow Dab's reins, a tall red-haired trapper with a straggly red beard to match and wearing a winter coat got out of the pickup and came across the road.

"Well, hell," he said to me like he was a long-lost pal of mine. I had seen him drinking in the Stockman's Bar in Bull Hook Bottoms with friends of my dad's, but I'd never heard him speak before. I didn't know if he recognized me from the bar or not. He had a marked accent, and I'd heard him called Swede in the bar. "I t'ank you for goin' over dere t' empty my goddem trap. I tot it was too dem' fir off the road fer 'nybody t' see. I figger I wasn' gonna check det goddem trap out dere in d' field today. But too goddem vet an' cold. Son-of-a-bitch, I figure 'nything in dat dem trap be drown' today 'nyway, lookin' at det goddem stream, runnin' dere."

I ignored him and swung astraddle Yellow Dab with the coyote pup in my arms against my chest. The little pup shivered pitifully and cowered away from the Swede's voice. "You know who the goddam enemy is, don't you," I said to the coyote pup under my breath.

"I s'poses y' din' tink t' brin' dat dem trap vitcha, now, di'cha?" I could tell he was getting impatient for an answer.

I said nothing but jumped Yellow Dab out of the ditch onto the road and stationed myself between the Swede and his pickup.
"You see me with any goddam trap," I said. "I spotted this little coyote pup disappearing into his mother's den out there, and I went out and dug him out. I didn't see no goddam trap."

"I s'poses y' gif me coyote fer me troubles 'n ve calls it skvare. I find dem trap later." He sounded a little less friendly than earlier. He tried to edge past Yellow Dab, but I kept Yellow Dab between him and the pick-up.

"This damn yellow horse is a pretty good cutting horse," I said amiably to the Swede, "and if he can keep range bulls and wild fuckin' cows outa the herd all day long, he sure ain't gonna let a stupid ass Swede by him."

"Anyway," I went on, addressing his earlier comment in a feigned thoughtful manner, "I figure we're pretty damn square already, and if anybody owes anything, you owe me for wastin' my goddam time, when I'd like to get on home and get outa these wet duds," I spoke in the same amiable tone I had used earlier but with a hard edge to my voice. I knew some goddam trappers would shoot you in a second if they thought you had raided one of their traps, and I didn't feel like taking any chances, especially when I realized the heedless way he was checking his trapline.

He tried to elbow past Yellow Dab to his pickup, and the beat-up .30-.30 rifle I could see in a rack in the back window. I kicked Yellow Dab forward bumping his shoulder hard against the Swede's chest. The force of Yellow Dab's weight knocked the Swede off balance to the edge of the road. I kicked Yellow Dab against the Swede again at the side of the road. Then, I raised my boot out of the stirrup and kicked him in the face with the boot heel.

He fell backwards to the bottom of the ditch and splattered into the mud and water there on his back.

"So much for your fancy fuckin' winter coat," I said, smiling down at him. His nose was gushing a bloody stream down the front of his coat.

I rode Yellow Dab over to the passenger side of the Swede's pickup where it was parked along the far side of the rode. I kicked out the passenger's window with my boot heel. Edging Yellow Dab even closer, I leaned off Yellow Dab's back and, reaching through the broken window, I retrieved the .30-.30 from the rack in the back window.

It was a lever action, so I kicked open the bolt and saw it was definitely loaded. I rode back across the road with the lever down.

"See this," I said to the Big Swede sharply, where he was on his knees trying to get up out of the mud and water in the roadway ditch. He looked up at me. I snapped the lever action into place. "Now, there's a slug with your fuckin' name on it in the chamber. You follow me or even come near me ever again in your whole fuckin' life, and this slug with your name on it is gonna find its way right between your fuckin' eyes and right into that feeble fuckin' brain of yours." I was laying it on a little heavy, I realized, but I figured a little threat backed up with the .30-.30 would probably back his ass off.

"Now, the way it would fuckin' go," I told him, lying in my teeth, of course. "I got a handgun of my own in the saddle bag here." I patted the saddle bag for effect. "You follow me or even show up anywhere near where I am, and I'll shoot you right between the eyes with that fuckin' handgun. Then, I'll stick this fuckin' sorry rifle into your dead fuckin' hands, so it'll be self-defense. They'll plant your sorry Swede ass in boot-hill and proclaim me a fuckin' hero for wiping shit like you from the face of the fuckin' earth." Of course, I had no handgun in my saddlebag at all, but I did have a .22 cylinder action pistol at home that I carried with me sometimes when I was riding my trap-line. Since I'd pulled my trap-line a couple of weeks before, I'd left the pistol in the drawer of the gun rack at home. "Shit," I thought to myself, "next time, I'll carry that son-of-a-bitch with me all the time."

I looked down at him where he sat back in the ditch water, looking pitifully up at me. Suddenly, he started to bawl with a loud whimpering cry. "I not folla, meesta," he blubbered around his tears.

"I got a fuckin' slug waiting for you, if you follow," I warned again, riding off. "I'll leave this piece of shit .30-.30 in the Stockman's Bar next time I get to town," I said over my shoulder. "You can pick the sorry son-of-a-bitch up there. I sure as hell don't want this piece of trash," I finished scornfully. "And in the fuckin' future," I added, shouting back to him at the top of my voice, "get your lazy fat ass out to check your traps twice a fuckin' day. If I hear you ain't doing that, I'll kick the living shit out of you again…only worse next time."

I was running out of breath, so I made my last comment to the coyote pup, "No reason for poor little buggers, like you," I patted the little coyote on his head between his ears, "you cute little bastard, sitting all day in a trap and even drownin' because that son-of-a-bitch is too damn lazy to check his traps and knock you in the head." I spoke this last part quietly because I figured the Swede would just take my comment as a sign of weakness —lack of manhood—on my part.

"Christ, it doesn't make much sense to kill something to put it out of its pain," I said with puzzlement to Yellow Dab, "when if you left it alive to suffer a little while, it might live a long life. This poor little bastard would be dead as hell if we had done that." I patted the little coyote on the head again and tried to consider the extent of misery that would justify "killing something, like even a human being, to put it out of its misery." I came to no good conclusions on that matter, so I let it go unresolved.

I trotted on down the road and into the yard at the school. I couldn't see the Swede anywhere back up the road, so I put Yellow Dab in the horse barn, unsaddled him, and made sure he had hay and a scoop of oats. He knickered appreciatively, as I left him and carried the little coyote pup into the school, along with the Swede's .30-.30, which I had slung over my shoulder.

I went through the entry-way and the cloakroom but could hear nothing from the classroom. I knocked at the door, but there was no answer. The door was unlocked, so I walked in. Nobody seemed to be around. I retrieved the empty overshoe box from the cloakroom and hauled it into the classroom and placed it by the pot-bellied heating stove at the side of the room. I got a towel from above the wash basin and spread it in the bottom of the overshoe box. I put the coyote pup down into the box as gently as I could.

"Maybe, you're a lucky little bastard after all," I said to him softly. "You got a warm bed here and maybe that trap hit you so high on your thighbone there that your leg's not broken." I held his mouth shut again and gingerly felt of his thigh and leg around where the trap had left its mark. I couldn't feel any break, but he was shivering so bad I wasn't sure. "I think you're fine, but I'll check again later just to make sure," I told him. His shivering made me realize that I was shivering like hell, also.

I also realized that I was totally exhausted—both from lack of adequate sleep and as the aftermath of a rush of adrenaline, following the run-in with the Swede. I found the coyote a few table scraps and tossed them into the box with him. He sniffed one tentatively, then wolfed it down voraciously without even bothering to chew it. He gobbled the second piece just as fast, so I found him a couple of more scraps and threw them into his box.

Then, I stoked up the fire in the stove and tossed in a little extra coal from the coal bucket.

"Shit, I'm tired," I said to the little coyote, as I curled up on the floor in the warmth behind the stove. I was asleep in about 30 seconds, but one last thought I had stuck with me even after I woke up.

"Jesus, Little Coyote," I said, putting my thought blearily into words. "You damn smart coyotes are the animal Tricksters, aren't you? The patrons of the human Trickster-Shamans?"

"Yes, we are, indeed," Coyote Pup said to me in a friendly voice, "and I have a bit of a debt to pay you for today's services, so maybe we'll try to work something out."

I was asleep before I could put any meaning to his thought or thought to his words.

Chapter 14

BACK TO SCHOOL

I was climbing a rocky mountainside, headed for a distant snowy summit that seemed endlessly far away. My Grandfather was behind me somewhere, urging me forward.

"You can do it, my boy," he said. "Just keep up a slow easy pace to the top. I'll be right behind you. When we get there, I'll lead you and show you what to do."

The coyote pup was ahead of me, moving without effort up the steep rocky talus slope. He bared his small sharp fangs in what could have been a snarl but really appeared to be a smile.

"What the hell am I gonna do?" I asked him. "I don't know if I can make it to high school or not. What am I gonna do about that? And how the hell much longer do we have to climb to get up this goddam rocky slope?"

He looked back at me with his jet black lips curled into what could either be a snarl or an inscrutable smile. "We'll see what we can do about it," he said mysteriously. That answer told me nothing, but I felt a certain amount of satisfaction in what he said anyway because at least it sounded as if he would be helpful.

"No more fuckin' trap-lines anyway," he went on to tell me, "I don't like traps, so if I'm gonna work for you, you have to give them up. Your younger brother is really jealous and wants your traps anyway. Give 'em to him with my blessing, and we'll all feel good about your action." He trotted on while I struggled to try to keep up with him.

"Lew, wake up, now, Lew," I could feel the hand gently shaking my shoulder as I dragged myself from sleep. I sat up on my elbows and looked into the deep brown eyes of Stephanie, smiling down at me. I felt thoroughly drugged and asleep. Despite the heat from the heating stove, I was shivering with cold. I squeezed my eyes shut tightly, then opened them and looked again at Stephanie.

"I was out for a walk in the beautiful spring afternoon," she said to me, "and the first thing I noticed was the overshoes box had been moved. Then, I found it in here by the heater with the most beautiful little coyote pup inside. He's even pretty tame although he snapped at me, so I didn't try to reach into the box, but I cut him a few pieces of the roast I had in the oven of the cook stove. It was nearly finished cooking, but I found him a rare piece that was still dripping red juice. I dropped it into the box, an he scarfed it down in one gulp. Then, I had to laugh because it was a very big piece and he had to burp it up again and chew it a little bit before he could get it past his throat." She paused and stood up to look down at me, her hands folded on the handle of her cane.

"My goodness, Lew, you look an awful sight, if you don't mind my saying so. I didn't even see you asleep back here until I was finished feeding the coyote. Then, he whined and seemed to point back here with his nose. I looked and there you were. I thought I better wake you because you were shaking like a quaking aspen leaf. You appeared to be freezing cold despite the heat billowing out of this heater." She leaned over me once again, where I was lying on my elbows, speechlessly looking up at her, for the first time regarding her solely as a woman rather than a teacher. I could now see better why Buddy was so taken with her. If you looked closely, her lips were pooched and full, giving her face an appearance of dignified eroticism, or so it seemed to me after my discussion with

Buddy. I had never really looked that closely at her face before.

When she stepped back, her small body also seemed strangely alluring, set off by the large bosom I had felt against my chest just the day before. I had to lower my eyes quickly to keep from staring at her.

"Your pants and boots are absolutely soaked," she said, bending over me again to grab my pants and squeeze a small puddle of water onto the floor. "You must get those off and let them dry at once. I'll get you one of my robes to wear while they dry. While you're at it, you better take that shirt off also. I can see it's wet to the waist. Just get all your wet things off and throw them into a pile there. Put on my robe and sit yourself down in front of the stove also and get yourself warmed up." She moved away to her small closet and retrieved a pink robe.

"You may not favor pink, but you're going to put this robe on and sit in front of the heater until you're warmed completely up. You'll catch pneumonia if you don't get those wet clothes off and get yourself warmed up. You look positively worn out. Your eyes are bloodshot and your cheeks are cracked where you must have frozen them. Where were you anyway? All this time. I thought you must have made it home all right when you didn't come back last evening. I never imagined you'd be out in the cold this long." I hadn't had a chance to say a word yet. I decided vaguely that her long discourse was prompted by surprise and nervousness—and by the fact that she was obviously very pleased to see me again.

"Now, you sit in this chair here by the stove," she said, moving a straight wooden chair over in front of the stove. "You sit here and get those clothes off and throw them in a pile and I'll hang them up to dry. And you get this robe on and get yourself warmed up. I'll go to the cooking stove and get the roast sliced and some carrots and onions and potatoes and celery I cooked with it, and we'll have a nice quiet dinner. And I won't even think of looking at you while you're disrobing, I assure you," she reassured me in her clipped teacher's voice. I realized suddenly that she was feeling very nervous and awkward, more so even than I was. I couldn't quite understand why. In addition to being glad to see me, there seemed to be something else bothering her that she wasn't mentioning—or maybe wasn't quite aware of or wasn't acknowledging. "Maybe, she'll tell me later what it is that's bothering her so much," I thought. Being an adult was more complicated than I had thought 24 hours ago, just before my graduation.

I struggled to my feet, stiff and miserable and, once more, freezing cold. My soaked feet felt like icicles again and I could barely take a step without crying out. They had become agonizingly painful.

After sitting in the chair Stephanie had provided, I wrenched as hard as I could to get my boots off, but I couldn't budge them. Bending down far enough to get ahold of them —even seated in the chair—was so painful it brought tears to my eyes, despite all my efforts to hold them back. I took my wet shirt off instead and hung it over the back of the chair. I sat in the chair looking futilely at the stove, tears poring down my cheeks. If I couldn't get my boots off, I could never get my pants off over them to dry. And besides, I thought, how would the swelling go down without my boots off, and would I have to sleep for days with my boots on—lying on the floor because I couldn't get into bed without taking them off?

"Now, here's some roast and vegetables for your dinner," Stephanie said, walking towards me. I quickly turned my face away. She placed a small table beside my chair and then set the plate of steaming food on it. I couldn't turn my face to look at her or thank her because, despite all my efforts, I was still dripping tears.

"Just a minute," Stephanie said, stepping in front of me. She put her hands on my cheeks and turned my face towards her. "You've been crying," she said with shock and concern in her voice. "My goodness, you poor darling boy, what a time you must have had!" She folded my face against her large bosom and held me until I relaxed in her arms. She kissed me on top of the head and then rested her cheek lightly on my head. She still smelled faintly of beautiful purple lilacs.

"I've absolutely never seen you cry before since I came to this godforsaken school," she said. "I've seen every other student here crying sometime for some reason or other, and I certainly cry enough myself, but I've never seen you cry even once before since I arrived. You must have had a really bad time when you left here. You'll have to tell me about it later, but let's not think about it now. But you absolutely must take those wet clothes off so I can set them drying before you eat your supper." She pulled my face against her breast once more and laid her cheek on my head, while she patted the back of my neck with her small delicate fingers. I breathed the enticing smell of lilac once more from her bosom, an odor that would never quite leave me for the entire remainder of my life.

"I can't get my boots off," I whispered pitifully, almost in tears again. "I tried but my feet are so swollen I can't budge them."

"Well, that's no problem," she urged me brightly. "We'll work on those in just a minute here. Here's my handkerchief. You wipe off your face now. I'll get a chair and help you with your boots."

She pulled up another straight-backed chair and, despite the mud on them, she lifted my booted feet carefully and with a great effort dislodged one of my boots and set it down on the hearth, facing the stove. She then quickly slipped off my sock before I could protest and was hanging it on the rack beside the stove when she noticed my foot.

"Oh, my goodness gracious me, your poor foot is a mess. You froze it, didn't you, you poor darling. I've got some salve that I'm sure will make it feel better." She retrieved a large jar of Corona antiseptic ointment and rubbed it over my foot. I couldn't believe how much better the salve made my foot feel.

"Now, the other one," she said, lifting my other foot and stripping off the boot and sock and setting them to dry. She applied the salve to that foot as well.

"Get those pants off now," she commanded. "I'll turn my back, Mr. Modesty. And then we'll hang them up to dry and have our supper."

And so we did, and the beef roast was delicious. During dinner, I stumbled through the story of my past 24 hours with some notable modifications and deletions.

"You better get to bed now," she said, after we had given the coyote pup our leftover scraps and she had put the dishes in warm dishwater at the sink. We also added a small bowl of water to the coyote's furnishings in the overshoe box. He snarled appreciatively but still cowered against the side of the box.

"And you simply must take a bath before you go to bed," Stephanie went on. "There's plenty of hot water in the boiler on the cook stove and you can grab the old tub that's in beside my bed. Or if you wish, it would probably go faster since you're so tired if you just used the big wash basin there beside the sink. That sink drains outside you know, so you can use as many basins full of water as you wish. I'll fill the wash basin for you the first time and then you can refill it as you wish. I'll get you a towel and washcloth and soap and shampoo and even some rinse. I'm going to be recording some grades at my desk but you simply let me know if you need anything else. I'm going to be working so you go ahead. I won't be paying any attention to you, so take your time." She hurried around gathering the items she had noted while I filled the wash basin with hot water from the stove. I had never felt so waited on in all my life.

After she retired to her desk, I decided to take her at her word. I stripped down completely and began to scrub myself as she had advised. It was a great bath. The soap and shampoo all smelled like lilac, so I suppose I did also before I was through. Since there seemed to be no urgency, I washed myself carefully and used several basins of hot water, as Stephanie had directed.

Despite her claim not to look at me, I saw her glancing up at me frequently and then letting her eyes slide by me when she saw I was looking, as if she were simply looking up from her grading. The attention didn't bother me although I was naked. In fact, I was proud enough of my young muscles that I struck a few dynamic poses for her, such as I'd seen in Charles Atlas advertisements for body building equipment. I decided to pretend not to notice that she was looking up at me, so she wouldn't be embarrassed about her interest and attention to my nakedness. From his box by the stove, I could see the little coyote smiling at me for how tricky I was becoming.

"You get more in life by being clever and tricky than you do by being only powerful," I remembered my Grandfather saying. "You must remember that trickiness is itself a power, so treat it with respect. It is one of the sacred paths of life and the most powerful one, so you must use it with care to help yourself and others and to do no more harm than is necessary."

I wondered if the harm I had done the Swede would be regarded as necessary harm. I decided firmly that it was. After all, he was running his trap-line in a harmful way, taking advantage of the gifts the animals made of themselves to him—and ignoring the pain he caused them on top of that.

As I was finishing my bath and drying off, Stephanie stood up and walked towards me. I quickly tied the towel around my waist, overcome with sudden modesty.

"It's all right," Stephanie said, smiling, "I'm not going to bite you."

She stopped directly in front of me and looked at me closely. "You look much better and you certainly smell better, too. But I am definitely not having you sleep in that cold unheated cloakroom tonight," she told me. "You could be very near pneumonia, you know, the way you were shivering earlier. We're going to have to watch you closely and you're going to have to take it easy and get lots of rest the next few days. Tomorrow we'll see how you are and I'm definitely going to get word to the school nurse to make a trip out here—to look at those frozen feet, at least." I didn't tell her that another expert, Joyce, had already inspected my feet and diagnosed them as okay.

"You're still just a boy, you know, even if you're big enough to be a man," Stephanie went on, reaching up to pat my bare shoulder. "You finish drying now and get that robe on. I'll make sure those wet shorts get rinsed and dried by the heater. And I'll get you another towel to finish drying your hair." She handed me a pink towel that also smelled faintly of lilac.

"Then, you climb yourself right into my bed over there and slide over to the side next to the wall. I'm going to do the dishes and clean up around the sink a bit, and then I'm going to read awhile. After you're asleep, I'll climb in beside you, and you'll never even know I'm there.

"I don't weigh very much," she added smiling and patting my cheek, "so you won't even feel my side of the bed sag when I get in. And you sleep as long as you like tomorrow. You need to catch up on your rest. I won't have you getting sick while you're with me." She went back to her desk to read.

I was feeling much better and went to say good night to the coyote pup. I petted his head and he didn't snap at me. Instead, he took my hand into his mouth teasingly and then released it, as if to say he could bite me, but he would try being my friend for awhile to see if it worked out. I rearranged the towel in the bottom of his box and added water to his bowl.

When I stood up, I noticed two small black fleas on my arm. I snipped them onto the hot stove and they made a brief hiss on their trip to oblivion. "Poor little bugger," I said, patting his head again, "we'll have to try to find you some flea powder."

"I noticed he had fleas and maybe lice as well," Stephanie said from her desk, obviously noticing what I was doing. "I'm going to have Mrs. Bradford, the school nurse, bring out some lice and flea powder with her…if I can reach her tomorrow. It's powder designed for children but it should work on coyote children as well."

I liked the way she called my new friend a child. "You'll be our child and we'll take care of you…so long as you teach me the ways of the Trickster," I said to him.

"What's that you said to him?" Stephanie asked. In messing with the coyote, I hadn't noticed that she was standing right behind me, looking down at the coyote pup as well.

"Oh, it's just stuff my Grandfather told me…from old Indian

stories he tells of the Trickster," surprised that I could tell the teacher something about literature that she didn't already know.

"My goodness, that's very interesting," she said. "Sit a minute and tell me more about this Trickster." She sat in the chair she had sat in earlier to remove my boots and directed me to the chair I'd been sitting in.

"Well, my Grandfather tells these stories where the hero wins out not by fighting and being stronger than everybody. He wins by being smarter and cleverer than others, and he is able to trick them into doing what is good and right without forcing them or hurting them. Of course, it often doesn't work out," I went on with enthusiasm. "Often funny things happen to thwart him from getting what he wants, and sometimes he wants the wrong things to happen and gets in lots of trouble with everybody ... when they find out he's been tricking them."

"My goodness, how interesting!" Stephanie answered. "I never heard of Trickster before, but he sounds like Ulysses in The Iliad and The Odyssey. He wins out over other Greek warriors by being cleverer and smarter than they are."

I had only read a paragraph about Ulysses in our world history text book, and I nodded in agreement, even though I didn't know what I was talking about. "Just being tricky," I thought to myself with a smile, which as it happened gave me away.

"Why do you smile?" Stephanie asked.

"I was trying to trick you into thinking I knew something about those Greek stories," I admitted. "But it didn't work. You knew right away I didn't know any more about them than that little bit we talked about in World History."

"Well, that was something that you did know," Stephanie said. "You know they were Greek and recited as oral literature by a blind poet named Homer. All that was in your book. In fact, I have a copy of The Iliad on my bookshelf over there. That's my favorite of the two works. You can read it while your feet are recovering from their frostbite. Go bring it for me so I don't have to stand up again on my poor sore leg, if you don't mind."

I padded across the room in my bare feet and pink robe and retrieved the book from her shelf. When I handed it to her, she glanced at it and then handed it back to me. "I'm sure you'll enjoy reading it," she said.

She stood up and walked to stand in front of me. She looked down at me with a serious expression. "There's something important that I wanted to talk to you about regarding your future, but I know you're tired. So I think it should wait until tomorrow."

"You're such a wonderful good boy…and so very smart," she said, embracing my head and holding my face against her breast once again. I turned my head to the side so I could breathe more easily. She tickled my neck with her light fingers and then ran them delicately across my shoulder and down my back, massaging gently.

"You must get yourself to bed now. Pay no attention to me. I never sleep very well, so I'll not bother you when I lie down later to catch a nap."

She walked to her desk with her slight limp, which put a catch in my throat.

I placed The Iliad carefully on her nightstand and crawled under the covers. I was probably asleep before my head hit the pillow, as they say.

Chapter 15

LUCK O' THE DRAW

Finally, I knew where we were. We were on top of Mount Baldy. It's the highest peak in the Bearpaw Mountains, usually snow-covered until late June or early July, so it must have been midsummer because the peak was bare, and I could see miles in every direction in the early morning sunshine. Square Butte and Round Butte in the Highwood Mountains were off to the west; the Little Rockies were straight east; and the three conical peaks of Three Buttes, more often called the Sweet Grass Hills, were northwest; farther away still and straight north were the gentle purple undulations of the beautiful Cypress Hills, stretching across the border to Canada.

We were sitting in a circle. I was facing a little north of east, and the off-white glow of the morning sun gently warmed my face, as it shined directly above me. My Grandfather was to my right, in the warmth of the south due to his age and wisdom but fiercely defying the powerful north by facing that direction. The coyote pup lolled on his haunches to my left, with his tongue lagging out of his mouth and a sinister smile on his face.

Across the circle from me was the Sacred Being that my vision had conjured up for me in the off-white light of the pre-dawn morning, when the world stands pregnant with all of the expectations of the future of the universe held lightly in its open palm. The Sacred Being of my vision sitting across the circle from us was none other than the legendary Thunderbird, most powerful of all the Sacred Beings, who controlled the destinies of all the sacred shamans and Tricksters who had existed in the past or did exist now or would ever exist in the recurring cycle of the future, time immemorial, and out of time and space across the entire realm of existence. 'The Space-Time Continuum' was a phrase I liked that I had read in an article in World Book Encyclopedia that rested on its shelf at the front of Burnham School. The space-time continuum is what I was really referring to. My animal ally and my Grandfather were in council with the Thunderbird about what would become of me.

"He is mostly an Englishman," the Thunderbird said in his quietest voice that still caused the earth and heavens to vibrate, "a detestable race of mankind. I cannot think that any good purpose could be served by an Englishman in this world."

"But he also has a bit of the blood of the Assiniboine Cree, who are of the most sacred clan of the Holy People," my Grandfather asserted, "and he is my great-grandson. We must not overlook that."

"Hah, even you are becoming too much the White Man," Thunderbird said sternly to my Grandfather. "He is your dear grandson; you are his revered Grandfather. There is none of this 'great' and 'once-removed' kinship in the sacred world. I especially detest those terms 'half-brother' and 'step-brother.' We are all brothers and sisters in this world. There is no halfway measures with respect to such things."

"You must also remember," Coyote Pup spoke with great dignity. He has grown much since yesterday, I thought. "You must remember that he saved my life from a man-made trap that would have pushed me before my proper time into the below-world through drowning, an excruciating death. Also, he meted out proper punishment on the malefactor that would have trapped me. He is brave and his judgment and sense of justice are sound."

"I don't know," said Thunderbird, "but I am impressed that he has the entreaties of two personages of such esteem as yourselves speaking on his behalf. I will certainly let him go forward with his apprenticeship, but I will make no final judgments until he has proved himself further as, I must say, I truly believe he will do." And then the Thunderbird rose vertically into the morning sky. When he had become just a speck overhead, he opened his enormous wings and flew into the morning sun.

"Don't worry," my Grandfather said to me. "He is just pausing in his selection of a future for you so you will be motivated to do even better and work even harder and learn even more."

"He would never dare let you down now," said Coyote Pup with confident irreverence. "He would not have helped you come so far if he did not intend to open the whole future to you."

I woke with a small start to see Stephanie in the faint flickering light of a candle sitting softly on the side of the bed. She was wearing a white flannel nightgown covered overall with pink miniature rose blossoms. She slipped off her shoes and then was working with something on her leg. I quietly watched her because I did not want her to know she had wakened me. She lifted the contraption onto the bed for a moment, then placed it on the floor just under the bed's edge.

"My God," I thought to myself, speaking to God with genuine reverence rather than profanation, "she wears a brace and nobody even knows it, unless maybe Buddy knows, but he didn't say anything, even in his story about seeing her naked. No wonder she wears such heavy dresses and long skirts. She must not wear that brace all the time," I thought. Some one of us would have surely noticed.

She continued to sit quietly on the edge of the bed with her head bent and the candle flashing highlights in her dark brown hair, now combed out for nighttime, falling in shimmering waves nearly to her waist.

She sat quietly in the same position for what seemed like an eternity, then suddenly her shoulders began to quiver uncontrollably and deep sobs wracked her body, despite the fact that she was obviously trying to be quiet so as not to disturb my sleep.

I was transfixed with overwhelming pity for her and rage at the unfairness that had left her with a crippled leg and a thankless position teaching in the loneliest of all possible outposts in the Montana rural school system. Unable to control my impulse to console her, I rose to my knees behind her and folded her in my arms from behind her back, my arms easily circling her small body and holding her completely enclosed.

"Please don't cry," I said pleadingly. "You are beautiful and I don't care about your leg. I love you anyway."

She tried to control her sobs and patted my hands where they rested on her shoulders.

"You foolish, beautiful boy," she said softly, "you are much too young to say any such foolish things. You cannot know what love is. You don't know what your future holds at this point. You are much too young to waste your love on a half-woman like me. You must save your love for someone you would want to spend your whole life with, someone that you could truly be devoted to forever."

"I could never find anyone better than you," I said pitifully, "and besides," I added, thinking of what Buddy had said to me, "besides I could never stop myself from loving you now, no matter what happened. I never want to stop my love for you. Love is not something you can think about stopping."

"You may be right there," she said seriously patting my hand. "But I'm sure you can love more than once. If you loved and lost someone once, you can go on and love again and again with no loss of the love that has moved into the past. Love is obscure, but it is also infinite...for each one of us, I am sure."

We sat quietly for some time, me clutching her desperately, and her patting my hands and speaking consolingly to me, even though it was me that had started out to console her.

"Here," she said, finally, in her usual controlled, throaty voice, "sit beside me and draw a blanket around both of us, and I will tell you what I was thinking about for your future or for our future...for the future, anyway."

I sat beside her naked as I was and drew a blanket from the bed to cover us both. We were both clutching each other's hands as if the world were about to end.

"My plan involves both of our futures to some extent," she began her explanation. "I am leaving the school here to complete my education degree at North Montana Normal School in Bull Hook. You are about to go there to high school, I feel rather certain, whether your father gives you permission or not. The law does say he cannot definitely keep you out of high school against your will.

"But I have spoken to him. He is mostly worried about the possible expense, so I told him I thought I had a solution. I rent an apartment in Bull Hook with two bedrooms, where my husband—ex-husband, that is—and I once lived. The extra bedroom has never been used. I had decorated it for a baby, but that was not to be. So if you don't mind wallpaper with candy canes on it, you can stay there for a very small rent because I am already paying the over-all rent anyway. The high school is within walking distance, the Livestock Commission is nearby so you could keep your job there, and we would both be finishing our educations and could meet every morning, and I'll fix dinner every night, and we can study together. But we can't, of course, go on sleeping together all the time." She smiled at me to soften her final remark. "This is a special occasion, because you were so cold...and because I wanted you here with me," she admitted with a giggle. I had never heard her giggle before. It make her appear very young. "And then you can go on and finish college, and who knows what all else?" she added.

She paused while I tried to control my absolute elation. Not only would I be attending high school, maybe, after all, but also I might be living with one of the four or five people in the world that I absolutely loved without condition, the others being Joyce, of course, first and foremost, and then my mother, and my younger brother, and, of course, Anne Marie, whom I was sure I loved at this point, also.

"You must think about this for a few days," Stephanie went on. "You must not make up your mind hastily on something that is so important to your future. You let me know what you decide when you are absolutely certain of your decision." I was already absolutely certain of my decision, but I decided I would reserve comment for a few days to give the impression I was thinking ponderously hard about it.

"So if nothing intervenes," Stephanie drew the conclusion, "we might both be together going to school in the fall.

"Now, we must both get some sleep at once. Morning will be

here far too soon as it is, and I must get to a phone tomorrow to reach the school nurse about your feet." She paused reflectively for a moment, planning her day ahead of time.

Then she turned to me. "You get back under the covers now and make sure you're covered up warmly enough. We can sleep in tomorrow morning, but we must get some sleep now."

After we were both in bed, we automatically turned towards each other and held ourselves in each other's arms through the short remaining night.

Towards morning, I was wakened by the banging of the school door being flung open.

By the time I could get my wits together and my eyes open, I saw Buddy and his father standing accusingly beside the bed.

"So, young lady," said Buddy's dad, outrage in every syllable, "this is how you fulfill your responsibilities as a teacher. I am on the school board, as you know, and we gave you a chance here. But now, I am not only going to see that you are fired, but I guarantee you will never work in another school. I will see that you loose your teaching certificate, and I will do my best also to get you expelled from college."

And so it was. I followed the train of events in an ever accelerating sequence. Everybody made sure I never had a chance to talk to Stephanie again in this life. She shot herself in her apartment in Bull Hook later that summer with the barrel of the Swede trapper's .30-.30 stuffed in her mouth. The back of her head was spattered all over the little bedroom with the red candy canes on the wall. The Thunderbird had definitely struck, I realized, although I don't know exactly what his decision was nor on what it was based. I guess he doesn't share those things.

I walked out on my dad absolutely once and for all later that summer although I was sorry to leave my mother and my little brother. I moved in with Joyce, first in her basement and then in her bedroom. I went on to get my education and continued to work at the Bull Hook Livestock Commission while I finished school. Mostly, we had a good life for a few years, raising her children, to whom I became devoted.

But she was jealous of my education and dumped me for a cow buyer that she ran away with leaving her kids. I would have raised them, but I could feel no commitment to anything after the loss of Stephanie. So they went to foster homes. I tried to get together with Anne Marie, but she would have nothing to do with me after the rumors got around of my disgrace with Stephanie.

Anyway, I pray and expect I'll be joining Stephanie soon in heaven or whatever the hell the alternative is, just so Stephanie is there.

The goddam little coyote—grown up, of course—still lives with me, at least part of the time. He disappears for days or weeks at a time, and I expect he's getting tired of being my friend, since I seem to be in no mood for friends anymore.

I woke up really then in a cold sweat. Stephanie was lying quietly beside me with her beautiful brown hair spread in successive waves across the pillow, her large bosom making a graceful mound under the covers beneath her chin.

"Son-of-a-bitch, that Thunderbird is sure raising hell with my mind," I thought, rubbing my eyes. I crawled over Stephanie carefully so as not to disturb her and pulled on my pants and shirt to take a trip to the outside toilet. When it came to pulling on my boots, I didn't have as much trouble as I thought I might.

I slipped my coat on and went through the inner door into the cloakroom, closing the door quietly so as not to disturb Stephanie.

When I went through the big main door of the school, I found Buddy sitting on the front steps smoking a cigarette, his paint horse's reins draped over his arm.

"Shit, it's about time you moved your lazy ass out o' bed," he said. "The sun's up and time'sa wastin'. Shit, you'll never make a jareen if you ain't up at the crack o' dawn."

"I don't fuckin' wanna make a jareen," I said sourly.

"Hell, I don't think I'd want to be a Marine either if I could sleep here at the school with Mrs. Swift—Stephanie—and stay in bed all morning, like you."

His remark startled me for a minute, but then I realized he was just pulling my leg. He hadn't been inside the school. At least, I don't think he had.

"Yah, right," I answered. I climbed down the porch steps and took a piss towards the morning sun. "Well, did yuh find Joyce finally, yesterday?" I asked.

"Yeah, she was just takin' a fuckin' nap, fer Chrissake, sleepin' it off. She better get used to the booze if she's gonna be married to the fuckin' Marines. Drink all night, and go like hell all day! That's us." He paused and studied the horizon.

"I guess we are getting married tomorrow for sure," he finally added—with some reluctance, I felt.

"You sure seem fuckin' gloomy for a new bridegroom," I chided. "Maybe it would cheer you up to know Stephanie and I are also going to be married…in June, of course. But I'll talk to her. Maybe, we could speed it up a bit and have a double wedding with you and Joyce."

"In your fuckin' dreams," he answered, stubbing out his cigarette. "Well, hell, Stud, what I come by for anyway was to ask you 'bout somthin'. I figured you made it down to the school here yesterday, so I thought I'd catch yer ass here." He paused in what I guess you'd call a pregnant silence.

"So what the hell yuh gotta know that you come to me for?" I asked. "How the hell can I help you, anyway?" I was mimicking some cattle buyer I had heard talking that way.

"Well, you ain't gotta help me at all, but maybe you helped out the Big Swede some. You know, the Big Swede that hangs out at the Palace and the Oxford and the Stockman's Bar." Buddy looked at me speculatively. "Well, the Big Swede comes by the bar where Joyce is nappin' 'n I'm sippin' the suds. Shit, he looks beat t' shit. He's got blood all down his coat and he's muddier than a fuckin' hog in slop. He gives out this fuckin' story in his fuckin' Swede English that no American can possibly understand. Anyway, he says some big young guy on a mean fuckin' light-colored buckskin horse bin runnin' his trap line ahead of him and stealin' his bounty animals, don'tcha know, out o' his very own traps. So he says he caught this guy fuckin' red-handed, but then he says the guy pulls a fuckin' gun on him, 's gonna shoot his ass off. So's he talks the guy out of it and is headin' fer his pickup when this damn miserable son-of-a-bitchin' guy sneaks up behind him and hits him over the head with a fuckin' fence post er some damn thing." Buddy paused dramatically to make sure I was following his story closely. What he said about hitting the Swede over the head with the fencepost made me think of Ernie saying he was planning the same thing for Lucien DuMont. Those bastards must get together and plan shit like that, I thought.

"So then this low-lifed bastard steals the Swede's fuckin' rifle," Buddy went on with his story. "And rolls the Swede's ass off into the fuckin' ditch er somethin', where he gets all fuckin' muddy, 'n shit." Buddy waited for a minute with a half-assed grin on his face.

"I don't s'pose you'd know anythin' about this mean fuckin' trap-line thief, riding a big buckskin horse, runnin' around the country with a .30-.30 rifle stole from a poor helpless fuckin' Swede, do yuh, beatin' people up and robbin' them, like the Big Swede ner nobody else counts fer nothin? God, what's this world comin' to anyways when you ain't safe, even on your own trap-line?"

I grinned at him a minute. "Now let me ask you one fuckin' question," I said. "Was this Big Swede, lyin' son-of-a-bitch, bleedin' from the back of his head, like he said, er was he bleedin' from the fuckin' nose and face from somebody that might have kicked the livin' shit outa him in a fair and square fight?"

Buddy's grin widened a bit. "Well, I know there's some silly son-of-a-bitchin' kid runnin' around the country who thinks he's tough enough to tangle with the Big Swede, who the Swede says outweighs him by more than double. What I wanta know is, does that fuckin' dumb kid have a brain in his fuckin' head. That Swede's fuckin' bigger than a house and meaner than a rattlesnake. This kid better watch his ass every time he hits the bars. Some Big Swede's gonna be lookin' fer payback time."

"What that Big Swede is, is scared as a fuckin jackrabbit o' that tough kid that beat the shit outa him fair and square, and he's now gonna be too chicken shit to even come near to that kid, whatever he may claim," I told Buddy with a touch of bravado.

"Well, watch behind yer back fer Big Swedes anyway," Buddy said, standing up and stubbing out his cigarette with his toe. "Jus' thought I oughta tell yuh all this, in case yuh knows this young thief that's hounding the Big Swede. I'd turn his ass in t' the sheriff is what I'd do. Can't be too careful, yuh know. Beatin' up Big Swedes from behind their backs today, robbin' their precious trap-lines. Fuck, if somethin' ain't done, it could be you gets beat up tomorrow—or me, or any of us."

"Not too damn bad an idea! Maybe the law should be brought in to straighten this out," I answered. "I'll sleep on that suggestion and if I run into this tough young guy, I'll sure suggest he contact the sheriff and clear his name."

"You do that," Buddy said. Then he did something that brought tears to my eyes although I would never admit that to him. He clapped me on the shoulders with both hands and gave me a quick hug. "You might be tough enough to make a Marine yet, sometime in the far distant future," he added, as he climbed aboard his little paint horse. "Tell what's her name, Stephanie, goodbye for me," he said riding away. He turned and waved once.

"Hey, Buddy," I yelled after him. "Is your old man on the fuckin' school board or whatever it is?"

"Hell, yes," Buddy called back to me, as he kicked his horse into a trot. "The old bastard has been chairman of the school board fer years."

"Damn," I said to myself, "the Thunderbird really is havin' his fun with me. I better get a fuckin' Dream-catcher, as if those fuckin' chintzy contraptions would work against a dream sent by the all-powerful Thunderbird."

Buddy jerked his pinto mare to a halt and turned back to me. "One more favor," he called, "I rode Paint down to Lucien DuMont's yesterday, and I'm gonna leave him there when I go off to basic training. I told Lucien Paint was your fuckin' horse whenever you could get by to pick him up. Shit, I ain't gonna need a horse in the Marines and I been seeing your eye on ol' Paint here, the little beauty." He put his head down on her mane and hugged her neck. "Shit, you just gotta let me visit her and ride her a bit when I'm back on leave, okay. I know you'll take damn good care of her, better than any o' these other motherfuckers." He embraced the pinto's neck again. "Right, baby," he said, kissing her neck.

"Shit, somethin' else I should tell you, too." He rode back towards me a short distance. "Joyce was gettin' in a confessional mood—since we was maybe gettin' hitched and all. She was tellin' me about her first two fuckin' worthless husbands, and how they were drunk all the time and weren't worth dry dog shit in the sack, if you know what I mean. And she was mentionin' some of her other flings, you know—with married dudes and cowboys and shit like that..." He paused and looked at me intently. I knew what he was gonna say. I could feel it comin' and all I could do was stare at the ground with my heart so high in my throat it was almost chokin' me.

"She said she had a fling in the sack with yer Old Man, there when you and him was workin' at the Bull Hook Livestock yards. But I guess you knowed that already from how you's lookin' there—with that fuckin' long face and shit. I don't know how youse wouldn' know since you was workin' there with yer old man every summer fer quite some years...and workin' with Joyce, too, a little bit, anyway," he added with a kind of wink. I wondered if Joyce had confessed anything to him about our little episode inspecting my feet and warming me up in the granary bed chamber, but he added nothing about it and, of course, I didn't ask. A tear forced itself down my cheek despite myself.

"Shit, you got nothin' t' cry about," Buddy said. "It sure ain't yer fault if yer Old Man has a fling in the hay. Men—growed up men, like we are now, after we's graduated—are just like that. Shit, it's a fuckin' man's right to get whatever piece of ass he can get aholt of, fer all the trouble we have to go through for them fuckin' bitches."

He paused, and then said the one word, "Women!" with high disdain in his voice, as my mother would put it. "Hell, fer whatever it's worth," he went on, "Joyce said yer Old Man was a lively son-of-a-bitch. Maybe you'll inherit some o' that pizzazz, eh! Like father, like son."

I couldn't stop the tears now. I didn't move at all. I just stood with my head hanging, crying my eyes out.

"Shit," Buddy said, with a catch in his voice, "you fuckin' think you got somethin' to cry about. Christ, you know what my old man told me when he fuckin' threw me outa the house. He told me I was a fuckin' catch colt, too, just like fuckin' Ernie. I was a kid my damn parents picked up cuz my mother din' want me. My fuckin' old man said he was fuckin' proud at the time that they adopted me anyway, cuz that made 'em good fuckin' Christians er somethin'. But he said he was sorry now they had adopted me because I was such a fuckin' disappointment to him and my ma. Shit, he said, they'da throwed me out years ago except it was their Christian duty to keep me till I was a man since they'd made the mistake o' adoptin' me. Shit!" Tears were coming down Buddy's cheeks now, too.

"Christ," he said, "we're sure a pair o' fuckin' grown ups, ain't we? —cryin' like fuckin' babies.

"Anyway, you're sure yer fuckin' parents are real, kid, fer damn sure, unless they fuckin' did a switch on yer mom, two days er so after you was born. Hell, I was there and saw you right after you wuz borned, and the on'y damn thing I lied about was that I said you was cute. Fuck, you were an ugly little motherfucker, then, just like you'll be a ugly motherfucker all yer fuckin' life." He paused, starting to laugh. I had to smile, too, through my tears.

"The only difference is you'll be a big hunkin' ugly motherhumper, instead of a puny fuckin' little red motherfucker with a squeezed up face. Shit, damn, I guess I should tell you the whole damn truth, then. I lied to you before. I figured you couldn't take the truth, but yer a fuckin' grown up dude, now, so I figure you can handle it. Yer fuckin' real mother, you know—the one I saw you with—was black as the fuckin ace o' spades, and she turned yuh over to what you think of as yer real parents a day or two later.

"Oh fuck," he went on, "I lied again cuz I keep underestimatin' you. I figure you can't can't handle the truth 'cause yer just a kid. But, fuck, you's graduated now, too, so you's growed up enough to know that yer fuckin' mother was Gravel Gertie, you know that fuckin' ugly squaw that lives in the dumps east o' Bull Hook…and bums drinks all over town. Fuck, she's the real mother I saw you with." We both were laughing through our tears now. We finally stopped and just looked at each other for a minute.

"Shit!" Buddy went on, "one item of real truth. We two, you and I, are the only fuckin' graduates of the eighth grade here. Ernie didn't graduate either. Before he tossed me out, my dad told me Mrs. Swift—Stephanie—had passed that report to him a few days ago. At least, he told me he was glad I graduated—even if it took me a coupla extra years. Fuck, the fuckin' delay was his fault. He kept me outa school half the time to work. Who the fuck can study if they never get to school? Fuck him, anyway." He looked at me, smiling broadly now.

"And fuck you, too, you sorry asshole," he said to me. "If you ain't a fuckin' Marine, you ain't nothin'." He wheeled his—or my pinto now—around and started away.

"Fuck you, too," I said.

"You know," I added to his retreating back, "the only reason they call you fuckers jarheads is cuz they use t' use fuckin' Marine heads fer batterin' rams. Marines' pointy heads worked better'n them damn big logs they used before." I paused for effect, but he didn't look back. "And there weren't no damage," I yelled after him, "cuz a Marine's head is too fuckin' hard to hurt." He waved a last acknowledgment without turning around and kicked his pinto into a lope.

I went back into the school to see if Stephanie was awake. "Maybe, it's just a part of Thunderbird's test for me," I thought hopefully. "Maybe, everything will be okay."

I suddenly remembered running into Gravel Gertie one night crouching against the entrance to the Silver Dollar Saloon. My old man was inside on a toot, so I looked through the glass panel on the door and saw him lushing it up with Joyce and some others from the crew at the Bull Hook Livestock.

"Shit," I'd said aloud, "he'll be all fuckin' night. We'll never get home." I turned to head back to the 24 hour cafe, where I was sipping green tea and reading a helluva good novel, Tender is the Night, by Hemingway's old rival, F. Scott Fitzgerald.

"You can be home wherever you are," a deep woman's voice said to me. I looked around and couldn't see anybody; then I looked down and spotted Gravel Gertie, who was looking up at me with her beady bright eyes. She signaled me over to where she was sitting and gestured me to sit down beside her. I joined her and put my back against the same wall that she had herself propped up against.

"You can be home wherever you are," she said again in her deep voice, sounding almost like the Thunderbird of my dreams. "All you need is Thunderbird's ambrosia." She handed me a large green bottle. Sure enough, on the side label it said, "Thunderbird, a fine wine, the Ambrosia of the Gods."

"Have a sip, young white man," she said, handing me the bottle. So I sat down beside my mother and had a sip of the ambrosia of the gods, named after Thunderbird, the most powerful God of all. As this memory floated in with the blessings of Thunderbird, I remembered his injunction on Mount Baldy about kinship matters. That's why I speak of Gertie as my mother as much and as dearly as I might speak of my own dear gentle Catholic mother, waiting at home for her drunken carousing husband and her most admired eldest son, me. My mother was a mother to all the sons of the world, as Thunderbird apparently saw it, and we sons were the dear sons and offspring of all the women of the world who wanted to be mothers. Women, I suppose, could beg off universal motherhood if they wanted to by not having children, but sons had no such freedom of choice. All sons had to have mothers, even Jesus, who could pass up a father—a father on this earth, anyway—but he couldn't be born without a mother, even to God. I pictured the venerated Virgin Mary as I'd seen her in a hundred portraits in my mother's Catholic materials, and I wondered if, as she aged, she did not look a great deal like Gravel Gertie.

"It makes you feel at home wherever you are," Gertie had said, firmly. "Without it, I wouldn't have a home." She spoke clearly and precisely despite her seemingly bad circumstances. She took a sip of Thunderbird from the bottle and passed it to me.

I wanted a taste, but instinctively I rubbed the mouth of the bottle against my shirt to clean off her spittle and whatever else. "No need for white boy to clean off the bottle," Gertie had said. "It ain't dirty."

I nodded in apology for my offensive cleanliness and took a mouthful of Thunderbird ambrosia. It tasted to my uneducated taste buds as somewhere between a mouthful of sweet gasoline and a mouthful of horse piss, but I swallowed dutifully. When she offered me another swallow, I begged off.

But I had stayed seated with her awhile talking about how Thunderbird purified her life and made it satisfying and happy. Then, I fled to the sanctuary of my 24 hour cafe and the rather effusive prose of F. Scott Fitzgerald.

"Shit, I s'pose I should pick up a jug of Thunderbird…if I was only old enough," I said aloud, looking to see if the real Thunderbird were in the morning sky.

"Hell," I went on, thinking to myself, "who the hell needs ambrosia when you got sunshine and water and the hint of green of new grass growing?" Little pockets of green grass were showing across the wet spring prairie that stretched miles in front of the school door.

"I'll give my mother a bottle of her Thunderbird ambrosia, next time I see her," I said aloud, thinking I would look up Gravel Gertie with my gift the next time I got to Bull Hook Bottoms.

I heard the school door swing open and the clunk of Stephanie's cane beside me. She put her arm through mine and took my hand gently in hers. "What's this you were saying about getting some ambrosia," she asked, "the nectar of the gods?"

"I don't need the nectar of the gods if you're beside me on my lifelong quest," I answered, echoing what we had been reading about Sir Gawain and the knights of old.

"Oh, Lew, you can be such a silly sweet boy. What a nice thing to say!" She tucked her cheek against my arm and smiled up at me somewhat shyly.

I put my hand over hers where it rested lightly under my arm. I thought, "All I really need in this life is Stephanie or maybe Joyce (or maybe even Anne Marie)." Then, I considered as an after-thought what else I would need for joy and happiness in this life, "...and Yellow Dab (or another good horse like him) and maybe a horse for whatever girl or girls I was with, and a bunch of novels by Hemingway and maybe Fitzgerald and Steinbeck..." I paused because a thousand other possibilities flooded my mind of things that might lead to bliss and future happiness in this life.

I turned to Stephanie then and folded her tightly against my chest. "I want to marry you," I managed to say in a strained voice, "I really love you!"

"My, you're strong as a young bull," she said, pushing me to loosen my arms a bit, but then putting her arms around me so I wouldn't get too far away. "You're still very young. You have plenty of time to think about love and marriage in the future."

"If Thunderbird doesn't have something else in mind for me," I thought with foreboding, "some test that might take me out of this world before my time was properly up. Then, I might not have much damn time at all."

Then, I smiled down at Stephanie again and gave her hand a light squeeze. Mindful of her comment about my strength, I was careful not to squeeze too hard. "Thunderbird will surely deal kindly with us," I said, "since you are such a beautiful, kind-hearted person."

Chapter 16

RECKONING DAY

Stephie—as she told me she liked to be called—and I ate a slow breakfast, topped off with her wonderful cinnamon rolls, something I relish, with a melted brown sugar and cinnamon mixture, whipped into a sweet batter and spread liberally across the surfaces of the baked rolls. I helped her wash the dishes and wipe up the table, as I often did for my mother, but I felt it to be something of a duty with Stephie, since I could do it so much more quickly than she could with her bum leg. By mutual agreement, she stood at the dishpan and washed, while I hurried about picking up and putting away this and that, wiping the little table, and feeding Coyote Pup, who now languished quietly in his box. He had licked his lips at the lavish meals he was receiving with no effort on his part.

"You probably take us for your dad and mom," I told him, scratching him on the head. "No one's waited on you this much since you wandered from your den, I bet." He only smiled a benign smile by way of an answer. "Your leg's not broken anyway, so you'll probably be all right in a few days." I saw that the gash and the teeth-marks on his leg were well scabbed over.

"After breakfast, we must hurry to the highway and use the phone booth there to call the school nurse about your feet," Stephie reminded me. "I don't know if you should try walking that far or not with your sore feet."

"I could ride down and make the call," I suggested.

"No, that wouldn't work 'cause I've got to speak to her personally about this matter and some others. I will try to have her reach your father as well, so your family will not be worried about you."

"Well, you could either take Yellow Dab yourself—or we could ride double, you behind me. That would save both of us from walking, and you would be able to speak on the phone personally," I suggested again, not entirely seriously, since I didn't think she would agree.

"That sounds like a great deal of fun," she said, excitedly "but I have not ridden for a very long time—since well before my accident, even—so I would not feel confident to ride Yellow Dab except as your passenger, behind the saddle."

"Do you have pants to wear, if you're going to ride astride?" I asked. I had never seen her in anything but long skirts and dresses.

"I have something even better," she said. "I will surprise you by finding my very own split riding skirt that I have not had occasion to wear in ever so long. I know exactly where it is, and I can be ready in a flash if you want to go saddle up Yellow Dab and get yourself ready." She smiled at me with genuine excitement at the prospect of donning her riding skirt and riding Yellow Dab with me—a real adventure after a winter of boredom and despair.

"I'll bring him around in no time, if you want to meet me on the front steps," I said, jumping up from my chair by the heating stove. Then, I realized I didn't have my boots on.

"We will have to put on your boots, won't we?" Stephie asked, almost simultaneously with my thinking of it. "I must inspect your feet before you try to do that. We don't want to take any chances with them."

She sat in her chair before the big warm heater and gestured for me to lift my foot for her to examine. I reached down first and pulled off the large stocking I'd been walking around in. She looked over my foot carefully, then rubbed on a liberal amount of Corona ointment—beeswax and sheep tallow, it said on the label, in an antiseptic base. It felt wonderful, I know, whatever it was made of, and especially fine to have her rubbing it gently into my foot.

"Very, very bruised, and discolored," was her verdict, "but the swelling has gone down a good deal." She pulled my sock back on over the ointment and gestured for the other foot. When she finished both, I had no trouble pulling my boots on.

"Good as new," I said, giving her an appreciative hug. She clung to me for a moment, as if in a kind of desperation knowing our seeming idyll had to end soon, in a good way or with an ugly crash was still to be determined. The Fates and Thunderbird had not yet coalesced on a decision regarding our futures.

"I'll meet you at the door with Big Yellow," I said, using his nickname. "Be sure to throw a scrap to Coyote Pup if you have some."

Yellow Dab was glad to see me as always, especially after he had spent the night all alone in the horse barn. He whinnied affectionately and nuzzled my chest as I entered the stall. I scooped him a bit of oats and saddled him while he was scarfing it up in large gulps. "You can't really be that hungry, boy," I told him, but I knew he'd disagreed because he whinnied softly and nudged me for more. "We'll give you another shot of oats when we return," I told him. "We have a special treat for you this morning, so I don't want you too perky on oats so you cause us any trouble. She is a very light load, I think—Stephie, that is—so I think you will like her as a passenger. In fact, she will give such class to our progress that I would guess that in future you would want her there a lot." I took my bedroll off from behind my saddle to make room for Stephie. As an after-thought, I slung the scabbard with the .30-.30 of the Big Swede's beneath the left stirrup strap, and tied it in place with the latigo strings. I pulled the rifle from the scabbard and made sure there were shells in the magazine but not in the chamber.

I slipped his bit in Yellow Dab's mouth and put the bridle over his head. I led him outside and jumped aboard quite easily after a night of rest. Almost no more stiffness, such as the day before.

I rode Yellow Dab around to the front door of the school, where Stephie stood leaning on her cane, her excitement barely concealed.

"My, he is such a beautiful color," she said, "and you keep him so well-groomed. You and Buddy take just excellent care of your horses. I am very impressed. On those occasions when they ride to school rather than being driven by Lucien, Anne Marie also takes good care of her little sorrel mare—Sunshine, I think she calls it—but Ernie doesn't seem to bother much with his horse. Forgive me, but Ernie seems to be a rather slovenly boy to me, although I feel sorry for him. It must not be a great treat to have two alcoholic parents, so that you have to be put in a foster home. But Lucien seems to be a fine father."

"Better than mine," I said impulsively, avoiding her somewhat reproving look at my remark. I felt strongly the bitterness of what I said and did not consider taking it back even at the hint of her disapproval.

I stepped off Yellow Dab to avoid her look. "Let us put your cane in the gun scabbard with the rifle," I said. "There's plenty of room for both, and I'll help you aboard."

"I didn't know you carried a rifle with you," she said, as I lodged her cane in with the .30-.30. Ordinarily, I would have been much more careful ramming something down a scabbard with a rifle, but I really didn't care if I returned the Big Swede's rifle a little more scarred up than when I obtained it. It was plenty marked up as it was. I avoided banging the cane into the gunsight, in case I decided actually to fire the weapon. That was about the only thing that could be too badly damaged by any hard use of that particular rifle, which was already dented and scratched.

Without giving her a chance to protest, I swept Stephie off her feet with my hands at her waist and easily lifted her up so she could straddle Yellow Dab behind the saddle.

"Oh, my," she exclaimed with a burst of sound that expressed both surprise and pleasure, as she grabbed onto the rear saddle straps for balance. Yellow Dab snorted disapprovingly at the unusual burden, but I had a tight grip on his bit and he knew better than to move while I was holding him that tightly.

I stepped easily aboard, swinging my right leg over Yellow Dab's neck since Stephie was behind the saddle. "Sorry I didn't prepare you more for that ascent," I said to her over my shoulder, "but I didn't want to give you any chance to disagree or become afraid."

She laughed excitedly against the back of my neck. "I'm sure that manner of mounting will be almost as much a thrill as the ride itself," she whispered just behind my ear. She dropped the saddle straps and put her arms around my waist and clasped her daintily gloved hands over my breast bone. She rested her cheek gently against my upper back with a wisp of her hair from beneath her ear-flappered bonnet tickling the back of my neck.

"Off we go, ready or not," I said, giving Yellow Dab his head enough so he started with a gentle trot. We hit a bit of slippery mud at the gate onto the county road, but Yellow Dab was used to the slippery ground and didn't even break his stride as he hit the gravel of the county road, crossing the east-west road that we had taken before, and heading south towards Highway 2 and the telephone booth.

A small group of prong-horn antelope dodged away from the fence-line along the road, as we passed. I slowed Yellow Dab to a walk, much against his will, so that we could get a better look at them as they ran away with their uniquely alert stance and then stopped and turned for another look at us. They were very fast runners and darted about so much that they were very difficult to get a bead on when they were running. But the wise hunter waited until their curiosity got the better of them—which it nearly always did. When they stopped and looked back, they presented an easy broadside shot, which if properly placed, pierced their hearts, and they had sacrificed themselves in death to their human predators before they even struck the ground, "humans, the worst of all predators in God's world," I said aloud.

"What was that?" Stephie said, against my ear.

"I was just observing that they are foolish to present themselves as such a ready target when they could have been out of range of most rifles if they had just kept going a coupla more minutes," I responded with my head turned towards her so she could hear what I was saying.

"Oh, it would be such a crime to kill such beautiful creatures," she exclaimed. "They are such wonderful, graceful runners, and their colored coats are so beautifully patterned, they must truly be among the most beautiful of God's creatures."

"Plenty of people do hunt them, though," I answered, "some for food but most just for the hell of it. They are pretty hard to hunt, but if they learned to quit stopping like that for a last look at what's after them, they would be almost invulnerable because they're so hard to hit while they're running. Their own curiosity—and their own natural instinct to check what's chasing them, to see if it's a real threat—betrays them. They should run and never look back."

"Good advice for all of us," Stephie whispered against my ear and gave me a squeeze.

I put my right hand over her clasped hands, holding Yellow Dab's reins in the classic way in my left hand, while I kicked him into a gentle lope. He was such a sturdy big gelding that his lope was much like riding a large rocking chair.

"Oh, how wonderful!" Stephie exclaimed ecstatically into my ear.

As we neared Highway 2 and the phone booth, I pulled Yellow Dab to a walk and glanced over my shoulder, "How was that little lope there? He's a great ride when he's loping, isn't he?"

"I think he's a great ride, no matter what," she said, excitedly, "but, even greater, is the wonderful warm spring day, the beautiful animals we saw…and the very special company I'm with," she added, squeezing me as tightly as she could.

"Better grab the saddle straps while I step down," I said, as we came abreast the telephone booth. I stepped down and lifted her lightly until I could place her directly in front of the telephone.

"I am constantly amazed at how strong you are for such a young boy," she said smiling at me, as she lifted the receiver and tried to attract the operator by clicking the receiver.

"It's all those many fork-fulls of hay I've tossed into the hayloft over the years…or forked onto the hay wagon," I said to her, smiling and remembering with a kind of bliss how she had peeked at me not quite openly but certainly with curiosity, while I had been taking a bath. "Well, we're not having any luck at all here," she said. "The phone must be totally dead."

"The winter cold and spring thaws are hard on these open-country phones," I said. "They almost always need service in the spring. We can head on up the road a little ways. There's an inside phone at the Fresno Tavern and Grill."

"That's a good idea," she said with longing, "but it's so far away. I've never even been up there the whole time I've been out here. It's just too far away to walk."

"Not for Big Yellow," I urged. "He can have us there in a flash and you can see where Buddy was having his wedding party, just yesterday."

"Oh, my goodness," she said, putting her hands to her cheeks, "Buddy's getting married? I had no idea. He didn't even give a hint to me at school."

"He didn't give a hint to me either, but I found out yesterday," I told her. "He's headed for Marine Corps boot camp in just a few days, so I guess he wanted to do the deed before he left the country."

"I certainly hope he's not being too hasty about all this," she said with concern.

"I told him my feelings for you, and suggested a double wedding, but he wouldn't go for it," I said jokingly. "I guess he thought a double wedding would be too expensive."

"Lew, Lew, Lew," she said with a shocked expression, "you two boys—you and Buddy—are too much for me. You are both so smart, but you never seem to slow down for anything, both of you, full-speed ahead."

"That's the Marine go-code," I said. "Full speed ahead and no holds barred. Charge the fortifications and take no prisoners."

"Oh, my," she said, laughing, "you can truly be so funny, even though I don't take you a bit seriously."

"Marines can't afford seriousness," I said jokingly. "Their lives are always too much on the line."

"Oh, my," she said, "you certainly are different boys than my husb... my ex-husband, that is, was when we were first married. He was very young then also, about Buddy's age but older than you by a few years. He would have been terrified at even the thought of joining the Marines or the armed forces at all."

Thinking about what her ex-husband had done to her, I didn't comment, afraid I would express my negative feelings towards him too obviously.

"Let's be under way," I said to divert the conversation from her ex-husband. She was ready this time when I lifted her astride. It was much easier and she seemed lighter because she prepared herself and dropped gracefully into her seat behind the saddle.

"I could grow to love being tossed aboard this tall horse as if I were a little girl," she said in my ear, as I swung into the saddle in front of her.

"You can try riding in the saddle if you want," I suggested. "You might find it more comfortable."

"No, indeed, I'm quite all right," she said, clasping her arms tightly around my chest again, as I urged Yellow Dab into his slow easy trot.

We passed the Empire Builder, the Great Northern passenger train that ran daily service right next to Highway 2 from Chicago, the Twin Cities, and Minot all across north Montana to Bellingham and Seattle on the West Coast of Washington.

"That must be very fun to ride," I said to her over my shoulder. "It goes clear across to the Great Lakes and to the Pacific Ocean going west."

"Well, I hope I don't have to ride it—or the local either—when I leave the school," she said mournfully, "I would have to leave so much of my personal stuff behind and get somebody with a car or pickup to come back later and help me haul all of it.

"Your dad was supposed to contact me to make arrangements to take me to town with all my stuff in his pickup, but I haven't heard a word from him for over a month now. I guess he may be having a hard time getting to Bull Hook Bottoms with the muddy roads."

"He leaves the pickup on the high-grade gravel road, so he can get to town any time he wants," I growled. I was going to add, "...so he can get to town and get drunk and laid by some whore any time he wants," but I thought better of it. Partly, I was silent out of regard for Joyce.

I would be fighting mad from now on if anyone even implied she was like a 'whore,' as Mac, the bartender, had referred to her just a day ago. But I hadn't realized he was talking about Joyce when he said it. I would definitely take issue with him if I heard him say it again, "even if I had to throttle him to quiet him down enough to tell him off," I thought grimly.

We were already in sight of the Tavern, just on the opposite side of Highway 2 and a short distance ahead. I slowed Yellow Dab to a walk. "There's the luxurious casino with the plush carpets, the chandeliers, the telephone, and the cheap booze," I said, smiling over my shoulder at Stephie. "I'll buy you a Great Falls Select if you want, or they probably have brandy or something like that, if you'd prefer."

"Whoa," she said, "how can you buy such things in there? You're not nearly old enough."

"The sheriff almost never gets out here unless he's called," I said jokingly, "and then he completely ignores who's being served since this bar is so far out in the sticks. 'If they can lean over the bar and see you at all, you're old enough to be served.' That's the motto of the bar."

"Oh, my goodness, you're so funny. I never know when to take you seriously." she said. "I never knew you had such a quick wit when you were in school. I guess you didn't have much chance to exercise it there. Too bad that school doesn't allow for more humor. That helps learning, too, I think."

I checked both ways for traffic, then headed Yellow Dab across the highway. I was nosing him around the corner of the bar to the rear stable, when I stopped him dead in his tracks.

"Oh, my Christ," I said, realizing even as I said it that it was the first time I'd sworn in the presence of Stephie, either at school or away. "Oh, I'm very sorry," I said, contritely, "I didn't mean to swear."

"Oh, Heavens," Stephie said, reassuringly, "you have graduated. I'm not your teacher any more. Instead I'm your very close friend." She gave me a squeeze to assure me my inadvertent swearing did not bother her.

"Anyway," she added, talking to me in a normal tone of voice, since the clatter of Yellow Dab's hooves had ceased, making normal conversation more possible, "profanity, swearing, all ugly language—even the f-word—have a place in human communications. Words like these help us express our feelings and our strong opinions so that others will listen. We just have to learn to use such words judiciously and with care in the proper company. If they are overused, they may lose their effectiveness."

I was so impressed with what she said I was stunned to silence. Her calm reasonable explanation settled a dilemma regarding swearing and bad language that had bothered me for years. My father hated swearing in the presence of women or young children. He generally avoided the f-word, but everything else was commonplace. My mother hated all swearing and would not allow it in her presence. Even if a guest swore at the dinner table, she would arise quietly and leave the room. Generally, I had taken swearing to be a mortal sin, as Anne Marie seemed to regard it, but one of those risky things that male behavior called for. Stephie's rational view convinced me completely, and I might almost say that I was determined not only to complete high school but to go on the college from that moment on. If that was the kind of thing they talked about in college—with the same completely rational approach that Stephie had taken—I definitely had to experience more of it.

"Is that the kind of thing you learn in college?" I asked her, with a touch of awe in my voice.

"That and many other important things." She answered me with what I took to be a mysterious smile, somehow hiding but somehow promising the rewards of future education.

"But what made you stop so quickly?" she added curiously.

I pointed to the green Chevvie pickup hooked to a 2-horse trailer parked in the back lot.

"My old man's outfit," I said tightly. "He must have gotten diverted from picking you up."

"He brought his horse trailer, also," Stephie noted. "He must intend to pick you up and take you and Yellow Dab both home the long way—by way of the Bull Hook bridge over the Milk 'n Honey River."

"I don't much want the see the bastar...," I caught myself and stopped myself from muttering "bastard," as I stepped off Yellow Dab and led him across the parking lot to the stable.

Instead, I said, "I don't much want to see him," as I lifted Stephie to the dry ground beside the stable door. I pulled her cane out of the gun scabbard and handed it to her. She touched my shoulders when I was close enough to her and held me transfixed like that until I had to look down at her, into her eyes.

"I don't know all the trouble between you and your dad, but I know you've disagreed strongly about your wanting to go to high school. But I think he has relented there. I really believe he has," she said earnestly.

"I'll believe it when it happens," I mumbled grimly. I led her across the grimy back parking lot, with its trash and dishwater mud puddles, whisking her lightly over any obstacles that might have impeded her or gotten her shoes soiled. I put her down finally on the little concrete block that served as a porch for the backdoor leading through the kitchen to the large barroom.

She held her cane up jauntily and pretended to rap at the door, clowning for me so I would get over the funk that had obviously affected me since I had seen my father's pickup.

"I'll be right back. I've got to take care of Yellow Dab," I said. "Just keep out of the way of that swinging door. The bartender—Mac, I guess he's called—throws his dishwater and trash out the backdoor, and he isn't too careful about who might be in the way."

I led Yellow Dab into the familiar dark stable, but I led him into a back stall away from the door, so no one could catch a glimpse of him without actually entering his stall. After throwing him some musty hay and a scoop of oats, I loosened his cinch and took his bridle off. Carefully, I shut and latched both the upper and the lower doors of the stall. Yellow Dab nickered his displeasure at being shut away in a dark stall, but for once I ignored him.

When I walked out of the stable door, my heart leaped into my throat at the beauty of Stephie's trim presence, waiting patiently for me at the entrance to the backdoor of the bar. I hadn't really noticed her split riding skirt before, but now it gave her an air of remoteness and sophistication that made me feel shabby and unworthy.

"That blue riding skirt is the most beautiful dress I have ever seen," I told her with a certain awe, as I dodged the puddles and trash across the parking lot. She seemed clean and perfect in absolute contrast with her surroundings. "It even matches your eyes perfectly," I added when I was standing in front of her.

"Do you think that's an accident?" she asked me with a smile, patting my arm affectionately, "It was purchased with that in mind. And I think Yellow Dab is the perfect buckskin color to set off my skirt beautifully."

Chapter 17

OLD DEBTS

Stephie took my arm as we pushed through the backdoor into the kitchen/backroom of the tavern. It was deserted but I could see the eternal coffee pot was on. "Do you want a cup of coffee," I asked Stephie, nodding towards the pot.

"That would be very nice," she said, looking around at the dirty disorganized piles of food and trash in the room with some amazement.

"It's all full of loose grounds," I said, as I was poring two mugs of coffee, "He just tosses a handful or two of grounds into the pot and boils it up. It gets pretty strong and you have to filter out the coffee grounds with your teeth."

"Thank you!" she said, as I handed her a steaming cup full of thick coffee.

"I always dilute mine about half with water," I told her. "Do you want any water, or sugar and cream in yours."

"No, this will be fine," she said, taking a sip. "Whew!" she added, after trying it, "I think I will take your advice, if you don't mind adding a bit of water to this?"

I poured some of her coffee back into the pot and diluted the rest with about as much water as there was coffee.

"I'll carry it into the bar for you," I said, "if that would make it easier."

"No, no, I'm fine," she said. "I only need one hand for the cane. Just lead the way."

She followed me to the large door that led into the bar. I held the door for her, and we proceeded into the large gloomy bar. We paused to allow our eyes to adjust to the dim surroundings. Across the room, sitting at the bar with his back towards us, talking in his usual animated manner when he had an audience in a bar, was my dad, his arms gesturing precisely and spontaneously to illustrate whatever point he was making. His only audience across the bar was Mac, the bartender, who acknowledged our approach with a glance but continued to listen to my dad's story with apparent interest until it reached some kind of conclusion.

"...so the way I see it," my dad was saying in his animated story-telling voice, as we took seats a few places away at the bar, Stephie sitting on the side towards my father and Mac, and me sitting somewhat obscurely behind her in the next stool. She hung her cane over the bar and listened patiently as my dad's story went on.

"The way I see it," my dad repeated for emphasis, "the open range is gonna be dead and gone in this goddam country, just like it is all across the state and, dammit all, all across the West. The last goddam area of open range to close up before this Sweet Grass Hills and river country up here was the goddam Judith Basin. Shit, when I was a kid, that was all goddam open country down there. You could ride from the Judith Landing clear the hell to Lewistown and hit hardly a goddam fence or a field. Now, for God's sake, it's all fences and plowed ground across there. Barley and wheat! Wheat and barley! At least, they still raise a few fields of oats so you can feed a goddam horse with it." My dad took a sip of his Budweiser. His drink was a shot of some straight-grain bar whisky, followed by a glass or a bottle of beer. In the morning it was usually a bottle, as it was now.

He had glanced aside and taken in a quick glimpse of Stephie.

He ain't gonna miss any girls in his goddam audience, I thought bitterly. "By God," I realized to myself with surprise, "he doesn't even recognize Stephie at all in her new attire and her riding bonnet. And I guess he doesn't even see me, sitting behind her." Mac took advantage of the pause to ask us if we wanted anything.

"No, thanks, we helped ourselves to the coffee," Stephie told him. "We'll just listen."

My father certainly needed no more encouragement than that to go on with his harangue.

"So now, goddam it, our open range is gonna close, too, goddam, all the way from the Milk River to the Cypress Hills in Canada and from the goddam Sweet Grass Hills east to Malta or wherever the hell it ends. I know it's sure a goddam long way when you're ridin' it tryin' to head a few heifers and old cows to the marketplace." He paused for a sip from his bottle.

"Goddam," my dad continued, "it's a goddam shame but you gotta move with the times. I figured I'd get a jump on the rest of the cattlemen and goddam farmers that have cows on the open range out north and get my stock t' hell outa there this summer and sell my range rights to anybody that damn well might want 'em, or give 'em away, or throw 'em away for that matter. They ain't gonna be worth a goddam thing in a year or two anyway. Might as well git out while the gittin' is good." My dad paused for another sip.

During the short interval, Stephie leaned towards me and whispered. "Your dad is very interesting, but my leg is killing me here sitting on this bar stool. Let's go to a booth where I can stretch my leg out." I helped Stephie to a booth across the dance floor catty corner to the bar. With a sigh, she slid into the booth facing the bar with her leg resting up on the booth beside her, while I took the opposite seat with my back turned on my dad's long-winded bull shit. But I must admit I was also finding what he said somewhat interesting.

"I wonder if he hasn't seen us or if he doesn't recognize me," Stephie whispered across the booth to me.

"Or he just doesn't give a damn one way or the other," I enjoined. "But his eyes aren't so good any more as they used to be," I added to be fair.

"So what I'm gonna do is send my oldest boy out north this summer, along with a coupla other hands, ol' Scott Kincaid that's worked fer me ferever, and some damn dumb kid that works for Lucien DuMont. Lucien's gonna give up his rights also and get all his stock outa there. He's been tryin' out sheep this year as an alternative crop, but I don't think it's goin' so well. Somebody palmed a bunch of young bred two-year old ewes off on him, impregnated much too young, so they're shit hard to deliver lambs, and he doesn't know shit about how to deliver 'em anyway, or any other damn thing about raising sheep for that matter. Well, maybe a few years o' learnin' in the school o' hard knocks, and he'll know what he's doin'. He really needs to hire somebody that knows sheep a little better than he does and fergit the help o' that dumb shit town kid. He's just sendin' that kid north with my crew to get him t' hell away from his old lady, 'cause he thinks she has the hots fer that kid. Jesus Christ, if you can't satisfy yer own old lady and keep her goddam ass in line, what the hell's the world comin' to, anyway? That's the trouble with goddam Lucien. He's a helluva nice guy, but he's too damn polite and easy-goin' t' get a goddam thing done that needs doin'." Mac, the bartender listened with seeming attention to my dad's story but turned from one job to another behind the bar, as my dad went on. Now, he began polishing a long line of glasses with a polish rag.

"So my kid's now outa school, just graduated, so I figure this is a good job for him." My ears were definitely perking up now since my dad had been including me in his story without—apparently, anyway—knowing I was there.

"You know I got some sheep, too, and they're doin' fine. Two cash crops a year, wool and yearlings to the market, so that ain't bad. But, goddam, I'm a cowman, and I, by God, wanta raise cows. So, goddam, I went t' the goddam banker in Bull Hook there, and I says. 'Mr. King Shit with all the goddam money in this goddam world, if you wanna make some more money, you go along with me. I wanna raise some goddam registered Hereford cows.' Hell, you don't want open range fer registered beef specialty animals like that. You don't run nearly so many of 'em, and you keep 'em around the home place so you can keep an eye on 'em. Every damn one o' them animals is worth a few thousand bucks and gonna be worth more in a few years. You don' wanna lose a damn one o' them er yuh got uh big goddam loss." He paused for a sip. "But fer every one o' them pure bred beauties you raise you got a helluva profit, too, by God. That's the kinda bull shit talk bankers perk up their damn pointy ears to," he added, "so you can damn well bet they was damn interested." He took a longer drag from his bottle and looked contemplatively at his reflection in the back-bar mirror.

"Anyway, goddam, I'm a helluva good cowman, best in the country, if I do say so myself, and I been cruisin' the country lookin' at Registered Herefords. Goddam finest most beautiful goddam cows on God's earth. And the damn bulls are so beautiful they suck your breath away. Goddam if they don't. Hell, my eyes get worse every damn year. It's gettin' so I can't see a goddam thing, but I tell you when I see one o' them damn Herefords I can recognize him a mile away, tell you his age, date of birth, background blood-lines, and how much he goddam weighs within five, ten pounds. Damn beautiful livestock!" Another sip.

"So I tells Mr. Shit Banker this whole goddam story, exactly the kind of Herefords I want and how many and what the market is and you know what he tells me. 'Well, Mr. Wetzel, sir, we like your idea fine, but we feel you gotta get polled Herefords without horns instead of the horned variety.' Goddam, I'm stumped, I tell you. I'm goddam near speechless. Range cattle without horns. The goddam fool is out of his goddam mind." A sip.

"So I knows what I gotta do. I lies in my goddam teeth. 'Yessir, Mr. Banker,' I says, bland as hell. 'You hit it right on the head there,' I says. 'Funny I never thought o' that. Goddam, guess that's why us dumb hick cowmen and ranchers go to bankers, huh? Cuz you goddam sons-o'-bitches know cows better'n we do. Sittin' on yer goddam lazy asses in them big chairs in yer bank all day, yuh know more about raisin' a goddam cow than a man that's run cows since he was a kid.' Goddam it, anyway, what horse shit! Well, I didn't say it exactly like that, but you gets the picture. Anyways, then he's nice as shit. 'I'll deposit that money in your account today,' he says, nice as pie. 'You go out and buy them goddam polled Herefords, and we'll be out to inspect them when the roads get better and write a report to our board for this new venture.'" A long sip and a short pause.

"Goddam, I took the goddam money he gives me and I goes out and buys the prettiest goddam string o' goddam horned Herefords, you ever did see in yer whole goddam life. Well, the roads been too goddam bad all winter and spring fer the bankers t' make it out, and I figure this summer most o' them Herefords are gonna be out on the range too far fer them goddam duded up bankers t' get a look at 'em. By the time they see 'em, they'll be on the market, and them beautiful goddam animals are gonna make 'em so much goddam money that by that time they won't give a shit if they grow horns out their ass. They're still gonna love 'em." He took a long sip.

"So what happens if the bankers spot 'em before that time?" Mac asked him.

"Hell, don't figger how to cross a goddam wall 'til you hit it—especially if there's any goddam chance it'll miss yuh. Hell, goddam bankers are so goddam dumb they'll believe damn near anythin'. I'll tell 'em I'm raisin' some goddam horned gophers er some goddam thing, that them goddam horny gophers broke outa their goddam cages and mixed in with the goddam polled Herefords and inter-bred or some goddam shit." He had several sips, as he joined Mac in a hearty laugh.

"I should make that telephone call to the nurse," Stephie said to me quietly, and she was starting to get up to do that when my dad's next harangue stopped her dead in her tracks.

"Well, goddam," my dad went on to Mac, "I was figurin' to get my goddam son to go into the Hereford business with me. Goddam, he's through with school, near growed up now, and he can do the goddam work o' raisin' these Herefords, while I'll supply the know-how and I'll make some money and, maybe, goddam, I might even start him on a little wage, or some goddam thing, if the Hereford business goes good." He paused and then his voice rose with indignation.

"The on'y thing worryin' me is his goddam teacher. High class little minx is tryna fill his head with big ideas about what high school can do fer him. Hell, the on'y thing school done fer me is waste my goddam time. Hell, I'd probably be rich and retired now if I'd stayed outa goddam school altogether. That little minx, crippled bitch of a teacher o' his, even come t' me a while back. 'Mr. Wetzel,' she says t' me, jus' sweeter'n shit, 'your oldest son is a very bright young man and a fine student. He needs to plan to attend high school next year. Bull Hook High School is a very fine institution, and it will prepare him very well to go on to college and get a higher education in law or medicine or whatever he chooses.' Goddamit, man, can you imagine a goddam son o' mine being a goddam shyster lawyer er banker er any goddam cowshit, beneath contempt, goddam job like that? In a pig's eye, that's gonna happen!"

"Mr. Wetzel," Stephie nearly screamed at him in a piercingly loud voice. She slapped her cane down on the table in front of us, nearly raising me from my seat. "You may address me directly, if you please. I am right behind you, whether you know it or not. And the first thing I would like to know is, why are you such a goddam liar? You not only lied to the bankers, which means not a particle to me, if that's your preferred way of doing business. What I goddam don't care for, however, is that you lied flat-out to me as well. When looking me straight in the eye, you told me you were going to send your eldest son to Bull Hook for high school this very fall, anno domini 1948. You not only lied to me, which I don't like, but you lied about your son's future. You would sacrifice him to your own petty whim, and that, sir, is goddamit, beneath goddam contempt!" She shook her cane in his face and stalked off to find the telephone. There was dead silence until well after Stephie entered the telephone booth to make her call.

"Well, I'll be goddamned," my dad sounded a little breathless, "is that Miss Swift, er whatever her name is, the teacher? I'll be goddamned, a mouthy little bitch, eh?" Mac put his fingers to his lips, gesturing to my father that behind his back there was still someone else listening. "Who's there, goddamnit," my dad said, turning away from the bar and getting to his feet.

"It's me," I said, in a very controlled voice, "and she is not a mouthy little bitch, or a bitch at all. She's a lady, but I s'pose you don't give a shit about that 'cause you treat my mom, the only real lady you probably ever knew, like she was shit beneath yer boots, too, just like you treat the bankers and me and my brother and Grandfather and yer whole family.

"You give me the keys to the Chevvie pickup," I told him forcefully and stepped up to face him, where I noticed for the first time that I was a couple of inches taller than he was and could look down at him. "You're too goddam drunk to drive, and I will drive Mrs. Swift to town with her stuff myself, since you promised you would do that, and probably never will get around to it because you don't keep your goddam promises any more than you tell the truth." I grabbed the pickup keys off the top of the bar and ran towards the door. Before I even got turned around, I was flooding tears, not for myself I realized as I slammed out the door, but for my father.

I had never felt so bad about what I had just done and said, nor felt so sorry for my dad, as I did just then.

Chapter 18

GOING HOME

I don't know how Stephie knew how to find me, but it only took her a few minutes to join me in Yellow Dab's stall in the stable, where I was crying my eyes out on Yellow Dab's neck. She put her hands on my back, making consoling sounds, then rubbed one of her palms up and down the back of my neck. This felt so good that I had to turn and smile at her rather foolishly.

When I turned towards her, she put her arms around me, "Tell me exactly what it is that's making you feel so bad," she said in a solicitous voice. "When you're grieving and feel worst of all, I've found it helps to try to figure out what it is precisely that makes you feel so bad. If you know what it is, then sometimes you can do things that will help make it better,"

"It's just my dad," I said. "I feel so sorry for the way he is sometimes. He can be such a really smart person—and even nice, sometimes—and then he can be such an goddam ogre other times."

"I know," Stephie said. "Sometimes we just have to learn to put up with things from those we love."

"I don't think I love him at all," I said fiercely. "I don't think I like him. In fact, I think I hate his guts."

She patted the back of my neck again with her delicate gloved hand. "Young people feel that way lots of times about one of their parents," she said. "I sort of felt that way about my mother, but then when they died, I realized I loved my mother very much as well. I had a special tender love for my dad, and the love I had for my mother was quite different, but it was equally powerful in its own different way." She took my hat off and ran her fingers through my hair.

"Well, I got the pickup keys anyway," I said, "so the old fool won't drive off the highway and kill himself. He's used to driving on a dirt road when he's drunk, but the highway's not quite the same. Anyway, since I got the pickup, I can haul your stuff to town, if you want to go pick it up now."

"Oh, that would be wonderful," she said. "I can get all my stuff to town at once and have a few days off before I start summer school at the college."

"Wow, you're going to summer school," I said, "a real glutton for punishment, eh?"

"Well, you don't have to go summers," she explained, "but since I took one semester off to work and see you students graduate, I'll be able to catch right up with my class and be a junior when I start fall term, just as if I hadn't taken any time off."

"So I'll unsaddle Yellow Dab and just leave him here with some extra hay and grain," I said, "until I can get back from driving you to town."

"I'll get him a scoop of oats," she said. "I saw where the oat bin is by the door."

"Oh, don't bother...," I started to say, thinking I could do it more easily considering her leg, but she was already on her way.

I unsaddled Yellow Dab and curried him down a bit, then made sure he had extra hay from the best quality bale I could find in the stack beside the outside door. I threw a few bales aside and finally found a good bale underneath the others, where it had been protected from the elements over the winter. I broke the whole bale and scattered it in Yellow Dab's manger. It was enough hay for a week. He nickered happily and ran his nose up my back to show his appreciation as I was scattering the hay from the broken bale evenly up and down his manger.

When I finished feeding him and filling his water bucket, I even got a padlock from the jockey box of the pickup and locked his stall door and hung the padlock key on the key ring with the pickup keys. I unhooked the old two-horse trailer from behind the pickup and pushed it into a parking spot at the edge of the parking lot. Stephie was already in the passenger seat when I climbed aboard the old green Chevvie, which I had driven many a mile. I only had a provisional driver's license, but that was enough to drive around "Bull Hook and environs," as it said on the limitations remarks on the license. I bounced the pickup onto Highway 2 and started back towards good old Burnham School, my old alma mater, as I was already thinking of it.

Stephie snuggled up against my side as I was driving, and laid her head lightly on my shoulder. "See what I mean about you boys," she whispered in my ear with a giggle. "You just really move things along. An hour ago, I didn't have a way to town and didn't know how I would arrange one. Now here, one hour later, thanks to you we're on our way to Bull Hook, and I'll be able to haul all my things in one trip, so this may be the last time either one of us will have to darken the halls of old Burnham School for quite some time."

As we turned left off Highway 2, I turned and kissed the top of her head, where it rested lightly against my cheek. "I love you forever," I said, quietly, but with as much conviction as I could muster. She said nothing but responded by reaching her right hand up to clasp my shoulder.

"Oh, look," I told her. She lifted her head and laughed out loud. A mother skunk and two baby kits were running along the shoulder of the road. I slowed down so as not to overtake them and possibly run over one if they dodged in front of the wheel. They ran ahead of us for a moment, then the mother led them down a small path to the underbrush beside the road.

"I will certainly miss all the wonderful animals that you see every day out here," Stephie said, "and the night sky I will miss very much as well. It is so dark out here at night with no artificial lights at all, that you seem to be able to see more of the heavens that any place else I've ever been outside at night."

We bounced through the mud at the gate to the school yard. I backed the Chevvie up to the door of the school, and we had her dresser and her treadle sewing machine and her clothes loaded into the back of the pickup in no time. The bed belonged to the school, she said. Her own in her apartment in Bull Hook was much better, so we left the school's bed behind. While she was sorting out the books that were hers to take with her, I went out to the horse barn behind the school and cleaned it out a bit, then took the tarp off my bed roll that I had untied from behind my saddle that morning and used it to cover Stephie's things in the back of the pickup, using tie-downs to lash it to the corners of the pickup box. I tossed the two blankets from my bed roll into the back of the pickup as well. I found two very clean fresh bales of hay from the hay shed and placed them on the opposite ends of the tarp to weigh it down for the trip to town.

"My, what a very good idea," Stephie said, as she carried a box of books out the big door of the school and saw my handiwork. "I was afraid my clothes might get dusty in the back there," she said, "but I guess you took care of that." I dropped the tailgate of the pickup and loaded the rest of her books.

The last thing we brought out was Coyote Pup, who rode with us in the cab.

"He can stay with me as long as he needs to this summer," Stephie said. "I'll be home every day and will treat him like my very own baby. I don't think you could take very good care of him if you're going to be riding way out north."

"Don't spoil him too damn much," I said, smiling at her and patting him on the head. "The damn school nurse hasn't showed up yet either, so I s'pose we'll miss her."

"Oh, my," Stephie said, contritely, "Thanks for reminding me. I almost forgot her. I'll call her from town to save her a trip."

We were soon on our way to the town of Bull Hook Bottoms as it was called. 'Bottoms' referred to the valley at the mouth of Bull Hook Creek, where it emptied into the Milk 'n Honey River. In that bottoms, the main downtown and residential area of the town of Bull Hook was built. The college, the hospital, and many new residential suburbs had spread out onto the gentle hills surrounding the valley.

By lunchtime, we had the pickup unloaded and Stephie's stuff arranged in her apartment, I got to see the candy cane decorated bedroom, where we deposited Coyote Pup with his box in an honored position. This bedroom was much larger than I expected, and the overshoes box containing the coyote seemed diminished in size by the room.

We went off to the Chinaman's Cafe for lunch. She had never been there because it was in the bar district of downtown Bull Hook, but it was my 24 hour cafe, so I wanted to take her there to sample the delicious Chinese dishes they specialized in. She liked the Chinese noodles as much as I did—or, at least, she said she did.

After lunch, I drove her home in the battered old pickup, which she said she was beginning to enjoy. She showed me her new Mercury Montego in the garage of her apartment. She had never driven since her accident, but she said she planned to get it out for summer.

"Come by and have a ride anytime you want," she said, "I'll even let you drive as long as you be sure to take us down for Chinese noodles again."

We finally had to part just inside the door of her apartment. I held her tight against me, wishing it could be like that forever. When she turned her face up to say something, my lips found hers and we exchanged a passionate kiss, she responding perhaps even more so than I.

But we finally had to separate, her "my dear sweet boy" phrase echoing in my ears for days afterwards, me hoping my "I'll love you forever" parting phrase was echoing equally in hers.

On the drive back to Fresno, I became very drowsy and pulled onto a wide shoulder area of the highway to rest. I curled up on the seat of the pickup and was almost instantly asleep. I could feel myself being transported to a large open green meadow with rolling hills and undulating with waves of green sweet grass to the pale blue sky filled with wisps of delicate white clouds.

A figure was jogging gracefully away from me in the middle of the grassy field. I ran after it but, while I could get closer and closer to it, I could never catch up. As I approached closer, I could see it was the receding figure of a beautiful nude women. Almost at once, I felt myself becoming aroused. Then, as I drew even closer, I had a startled sense of recognition, but it was only when the figure glanced back at my pursuit that I realized the running nude woman was my own dear mother.

The realization of who it was startled me awake in a cold sweat. There were tears running uncontrollably down my cheeks.

"Goddam you, Thunderbird," I screamed at the sun. "Get your claws out of my brain."

After my tears cleared, I restarted the pickup and pulled carefully back onto the highway. I didn't want any more unexpected tricks from Thunderbird.

When I got back to the Fresno Bar and Tavern, I backed the pickup up in front of the horse trailer, where I had parked. I didn't hook it up, but I took the two bales of hay I'd picked up at the school and placed them in Yellow Dab's stall. I refilled his water bucket and tossed him a little scoop of oats. He nickered his appreciation as I broke a little of the better hay out of a bale and put it on top of his other hay. The better hay was blue joint, the finest grass and most nutritious hay available on the face of the earth. It grew here and there along the river valley and throughout the region of the Sweet Grass Hills. The name 'sweet grass' came from its light blue beauty and the abundance of blue joint throughout the area. The bales I had taken from the school for Yellow Dab came from our own ranch in the Milk 'n Honey Valley.

Inside the bar my dad was still spinning out his endless stories to Mac. I saw he had switched to drinking coffee, which was a good sign that he was getting ready to go. The Big Swede was sitting next to my dad at the bar with his back to the door, listening of course to my dad. In case there might be trouble with the Swede, I didn't want my father in the middle of it, so I sat down on the stool right next to the Swede but which was behind his back, due to the way he was sitting listening to my father. I removed the key to the padlock on the door to Yellow Dab's stall from the ring and slid the pickup keys along the bar in front of the Swede so they rested on the bar in front of my dad.

"Did you fuckin' pull your goddam trap-line like I told you to, you foul-smelling piece of tripe," I said to the Big Swede evenly behind his back, just loud enough so he would be sure to hear. "Or do I have to kick your lazy fat ass around the parking lot here, too, 'cause you don't take care of your trapline like a decent trapper oughta?"

I had a Budweiser beer bottle held lightly in my hand, cocked and ready to land where I'd kicked him in the nose the day before, but I didn't have to use it. He turned around when I spoke, and when he saw who it was, he put up his hands and cowered away.

"I's do eet right 'way," he squeaked, hurrying out the door. Mac smiled knowingly. He had figured out what was going on and who was the probable alleged trap-line thief.

"Goddam," my dad said mildly, "I've tried to get rid of that smelly old fart fer years, and you take care of it in thirty seconds. How the hell d'ya manage that?" My dad was talking past me, and he wouldn't look at me, but what he said was obviously addressed to me—and in an amiable tone of voice.

"Well, did you get Miss Swift delivered with her shit to Bull Hook this morning? She should be goddam happy. She's gettin' a bigger check than she expected here in a couple of days since she did such a good job there fer the school in the emergency. We decided to give her a bonus. I talked to Morrises and they want to talk her into staying on next year, but I figure she's long gone. I don't think she'll go for another year, and besides yer aunt's gonna be ready to go back to work teaching at Burnham in the fall, I think. I sure hope so. I'm gettin' goddam tired of havin' her moping around the house at the ranch there. Shit, I never did get along with that prissy bitch, even if she's my oldest sister. God, she's boring as a fence post. That's what goddam high school and college did fer her."

"Grandma's not boring and she went to high school and Mom graduated, too, and she's not boring," I said. "Or maybe you goddam think so," I said, looking at him for the first time directly, as a kind of challenge, but keeping my voice low and even. "'Cause if you do, you should tell me so right here and now; 'cause if you do I plan to knock the livin' shit outa you right here and now."

"I s'pose you really mean that, don't you, kid," he said in a calm voice, facing me for the first time. I knew exactly what to expect. I had seen him fight too many times in barroom brawls not to be ready. His right-handed sucker punch was already headed for my face, a long upper cut from under the bar.

I simply stepped back and his punch whizzed by in front of my nose. If it had hit me in the face, I thought, I'd have been out colder than a mackerel, and he would have wiped his bloody knuckles and ordered a drink for the house to celebrate his victory. I'd seen it often enough.

Instead, the momentum of his punch almost tipped him off the stool he was perched on. And I had dodged behind him where he sat. I pushed as hard against his back as I could. My push and the force of his momentum tipped him and the stool into a tangled mess on the floor. He knew what was coming next, also, but too much booze and failing eyesight, and maybe a bit of aging and lack of recent practice with barroom brawling betrayed him.

The heel of my boot was headed straight into his nose. He managed to dodge that but I anticipated the way he would go, and my heel landed squarely on his Adam's apple. He gurgled and turned purple and rolled around the floor, trying to catch his breath.

"Drinks for the goddam house," I said loudly, so my dad would be sure to hear, in whatever state he might be in. I turned my back on him and faced the bar, as I'd often seen him do under similar circumstances.

"Christ! he might really be hurt," Mac said, looking over the bar with a worried expression.

"Shit, he's too mean to be fuckin' hurt," I said evenly, echoing an expression I'd often heard from my dad. I kept my voice dispassionate, refusing to allow myself to feel sorry for my father again, as I had that morning. "I ain't gonna cry like the fuckin' weak-kneed wimp I was this morning," I said to myself.

"'Course I ain't really hurt," I heard the voice behind me say, but still with a strange croaking tone. I didn't even have to glance in the barroom mirror to know what to expect. When I glanced in the mirror, I saw the bar stool high overhead descending my way. But I wasn't there anymore. The bar stool smashed on the top of the bar at about the same time as my boot heel landed against the tendon behind my old man's knee joint.

When he hit the floor this time, he was a little too tired to dodge, and my boot heel caught him square in the nose, where I'd had it aimed before but missed. He was stalled out this time for sure. He was conscious but there was a shadow of fear in his face that I had never seen there before. He looked up at me with somewhat glassy eyes, but his back seemed glued to the floor. His head was propped up at kind of an angle against the bar rail.

"Jesus, could be a broken nose," Mac said from behind the bar, but he knew my blood was up, so he didn't make a move to come out from behind the bar.

I was a little proud. I had beaten the Kung Fu Master of barroom brawling at his own game. "The goddam son-of-a-bitch that wrote the book on brawls goes down," I said to Mac, as he served me a beer on the house. "He al'ays fuckin' told me: Get 'em on the floor by whatever fuckin' means; then put the boots to 'em. Go for the face first er the gut. If yuh really gotta grudge on the son-of-a-bitch, go fer the balls, and kick the shit outa whatever you go for 'til the goddam son-of-a-bitch ain't comin' back fer more," I took a sip of the bar draft beer, which at least was moist.

Buddy and Joyce came banging through the front door, just then. Buddy yelled, "By God, we finally did it. We finally tied the knot fer good and all. By God, and we can drink all night 'cause I gotta catch a bus fer a physical in Butte at noon tomorrow."

They were both bouncing their way up to the bar when they almost simultaneously spotted the old man. Joyce screamed, putting her hands over her mouth. She ran to kneel beside him to see what she could do to help.

"The old son-of-a-bitch swung on the kid first," Mac said, from behind the bar. "It was a fuckin' fair and square fight and the kid beat the livin' shit outa him." His voice held a note of awe, I thought.

"Christ, Buddy," I said, holding his arm, "I hope I din't hurt the old bastard too much." I glanced back at where my dad was still stretched out on the floor, Joyce gently wiping the blood from his face, carefully avoiding his broken nose.

"Give him a hand, would ya?" I said to Buddy with a croak in my voice. "He'll probably need it, for his broken nose if nothin' else."

Buddy just nodded and put his arm around my shoulder. "We'll take care of it," he said. "You just as well get the hell outa here. The sheriff may show up if we haul him to the hospital."

"Tell the old bastard I'll be at Lucien DuMont's, figurin' out how to move them fuckin' cows off the open range," I said. I was feelin' better but thought I might not see Buddy for awhile. "I guess the Old West is pretty well dead...," I added, "but the fuckin' Marines go on forever." I gave Buddy a quick hug and was out the door.

Yellow Dab was ecstatic to see me after spending the whole day in the dark stall. I put the padlock and key from my old man's pickup into my pocket in case I needed them again.

After we'd saddled up, Big Yellow and I headed across Highway 2 and across the tracks of the Great Northern, on the way to Lucien's place. The sunset in the west was sending brilliant crimson flashes across the prairie. The whole sky and the whole landscape seemed to be in movement with flashing crimson lights and shadows.

I gave Yellow Dab his head and he hit a fast trot. I was looking forward to seeing how the young ewe and the lamb I'd delivered were coming along. And I had to admit to myself that I was really longing to see Anne Marie again and touch her hand and catch a glimpse of her trim, beautifully arched bare feet. I smiled. Maybe, she could come and help us round up cows from the open country to the north this summer. That would make it a hell of a lot more pleasant summer than spending it just in the company of Old Scott and that fuckin' sourpuss Ernie. Old Scott was great fun, but Ernie was a true pain-in-the-ass.

Anne Marie might just make it all right.

I thought I heard Coyote Pup howl at the rising moon, but it probably was one of his brothers.

William W. Thackeray, Senior Professor at Montana State University–Northern in Havre, Montana, was born on a ranch in north-central Montana and began his education at Burnham School, a rural school that is still standing twenty some miles west of Havre. Havre itself was known as Bull Hook Bottoms until it was renamed by James J. Hill, who wanted a more dignified name for the northern Montana headquarters of the Great Northern Railroad he was building to the Pacific Coast.